THE
RELENTLESS
GUN

THE RELENTLESS GUN

•

Pete Peterson

AVALON BOOKS
NEW YORK

PRINTED IN THE UNITED STATES OF AMERICA
ON ACID-FREE PAPER
BY HADDON CRAFTSMEN, BLOOMSBURG, PENNSYLVANIA

To my wife Margaret
for her support;
and to my little pard, Evan,
who keeps me young.

Chapter One

Young Jack Dancer regarded his image in the oval mirror hanging by a square-headed nail in the wall above the washstand. He moved his head a little to the right to rescue his reflection from the crazing of the silvered backing of the glass. Licking his fingers, he attempted to plaster down the stubborn stalk of ash blond hair that sprang from the crown of his head like a prairie dog out of its hole. He reached into the top drawer of the chest and, digging his hand under the folded clothes, Jack extracted a small glass bottle half-filled with bay rum, a gift last Christmas from his Uncle John. He poured a pool of the fragrance into his palm and splashed it freely on his whiskerless cheeks, then checked the mirror again, frowning at the cluster of pimples on his chin. He shrugged, smoothed the bib of his overalls, and hurried from the room.

It was Saturday, and Jack was going into town. Rushing through the kitchen, he stepped onto the sleeping porch, thrust open the screen door, and bounded into the farmyard. Spying his mother at the clothesline, he halted in mid-leap and leaned back to catch the door before it slammed shut, thereby avoiding the shouted reprimand the noise would

1

generate. Then, resuming his stride, Jack rushed to the barn and led Old Gray out of the stall, having saddled up before going inside to clean up. He swung into the leather saddle and walked the gelding from the hardpack of the farmyard, then urged it to a trot.

Holding the tattered corner of a towel to the line with one hand and pulling the clothespins from her mouth with the other, Grace Dancer shouted after her son. Jack pretended not to hear and rode on without turning his head.

Twisting his face, he pulled at the crotch of his threadbare overalls in an attempt to relieve the bind that sitting a saddle caused. As his ma said, his clothes "fit too soon." A gangly specimen of seventeen, at at half-inch over six feet, the boy was already taller than his pa had been. The sleeves of his homespun shirt barely extended below his elbows and the legs of his trousers stopped two inches shy of the tops of his coarse farmer's brogans, indicating a recent spurt of growth.

Jack pulled the brim of a slouch hat down over his brown eyes, an attempt to intercept the blinding shafts of the setting sun that darted unimpeded by tree or structure over the rolling plain of North Texas, now alive with the riotous panoply of spring wildflowers. Busy imagining, in thrilling detail, how his visit to town would play out, he was unmindful of the trill of the meadowlark or the drone of the bee as those creatures worked late to extract a living from the blooming carpet of bluebonnet, buttercup, and Indian paintbrush in his path. He took no notice of the jacks and cottontails that parted the tall grasses, scampering to escape the plodding hooves of the gelding.

As he climbed the gentle slope that kept the town from sight, his mother's shouted admonition repeated itself for his conscience to consider.

"Stay out of trouble, Little Jack, and away from the saloons."

But Jack had already figured that it wouldn't hurt a darn thing to have a beer or two. He had earned it, working hard at the plowing and spring planting. Jack hated the farm, and he eagerly awaited the fall, after the crops were in, when his Uncle John would come riding in to take him along on a wild horse roundup. The annual horse hunt had become the lone highlight of his year.

Buffalo Springs was not much of a town. Four saloons, two stores, a horse barn, and a gunsmith's shop. It was a supply point on the Chisholm Trail for the herds headed north across the Indian Nations for the railheads in Kansas. But it *was* a town—Jack's only available diversion between here and Fort Worth.

As he rode down the knoll to the street, Jack regarded the cribs behind the saloons—one-room shacks, thrown together with raw lumber—where the passing trailhands or local Lotharios took the girls from the noisy bars to enjoy some privacy. He blushed at the images floating in his head. It was a curiosity he had yet to satisfy. The only female form that Jack had ever seen that was not fully clothed was in the Montgomery Ward wishbook that time he had gotten hold of it before his ma tore those pages out. It was a thing that had been on his mind more and more in the last couple of years.

Jack brought Old Gray to a halt in front of the Golden Calf as he swung a long leg over the horn of his saddle and slid off the horse's side to the ground. As he wrapped the reins around the hitchrail, he calculated the number of horses standing hipshot in front of the four drinking establishments and decided there must be a herd somewhere close by. The sun had only just dropped behind the tops of the cottonwoods at the end of the street, but the tinny strains of pianos and the first hesitant laughs from the throats of men beginning to loosen after a hard, dusty day

were already trickling through the batwing doors into the
street.

Peering over the top of the sectioned door, Jack surveyed
the room. Cowboys were lined shoulder to shoulder at the
wooden bar, their faces streaked with the miles of trail they
had traveled. A smoky fog had begun to obscure the ceiling. One drover leaned lazily against an old spinet against
the far wall, gripping a glass of rye in one grimy fist as he
tried to pick out a tune around the missing keys on the
yellowed keyboard with the other hand. The smell that
drifted over to Jack at the door was an admixture: the
slightly sour odor of beer and sweat, smoke and leather, a
hint of cheap perfume, and the sawdust that blanketed the
floor. He felt a tingle of excitement as he pushed his way
into the dim interior.

Jack ordered a beer at the bar, then carried it to the rear
of the saloon where there was a billiard table. He set his
beer on a rail on the wall and picked a cue off the rack.
He chalked the tip and dug into a corner pocket of the table
for the cue ball. He bounced the white ball off the opposite
cushion a few times with the cue stick, testing his English,
then turned to reach for his beer mug. Jack jumped, not
having been aware of the girl standing behind him.

"Hi. I'm Abby. Want to shoot a game?"

Jack flushed and nodded, moving back against the wall
while she racked the balls. Abby slid the rack into its niche
under the table and walked up to Jack, pressing herself
firmly against him and grabbing hold of his cue stick.

"Can I use your pole?"

Jack swallowed hard and handed her the cue, trying to
act as if this sort of exchange happened to him every day.
Her perfume hung in a cloud around him. He filled his
lungs, trying to inhale it all before it got away.

Abby bent over the table and sent the clustered balls
scattering with a loud crack. Two stripes dropped on the

break. She was positioning herself for her second shot when four men burst noisily through the door at the front of the saloon. The girl frowned when she recognized them, then turned back to the table.

Jack knew them too. The McCabe brothers. They were ruffians and bullies, always running roughshod over those weaker than themselves, and their daddy owned most of this part of Texas. Jack watched as two of them, Cash and Gunter, made their way toward the pool table.

The young farmer had to admit that Cash McCabe was a handsome man. He dressed a lot better than many other folks did in these parts, for sure. A real peacock. And he was big—six-one and about two hundred and ten pounds—with black hair and a black mustache, and gray eyes cold enough to kill crops. At twenty-two, he was the youngest of the McCabes, and the most brazen. Cash had a bent toward pushing folks, knowing his brothers were there to back him.

Gunter was the one that sent a chill up Jack's backbone, though. He was not big, only about five-eight and likely did not weigh over one forty-five. But he was an albino, no color to the man at all. His hair hung down to his shoulders, white as a fresh-washed sheet on a line. Eyebrows too. Gunter's cheeks had never seen a razor and were smoother than Jack's own. And his skin was moon-pale, with a funny kind of pink cast to it. He went bundled up during the day in long sleeves and a big scarf, for he could not abide the sun. And he always wore those dark spectacles, so that a man couldn't see his eyes. Gunter was mean-spirited and sneaky, resenting the visible fact that he was different and smaller than his brothers.

Abby leaned over to shoot at the nine-ball that was hanging in the side pocket, her back to the approach of Cash McCabe. He stopped behind her, swatted her smartly on the rump, and grabbed the butt of her cue. She whirled and straightened, her eyes crackling.

"Come on, Abby, I'll buy you a drink before we go out back."

She freed the cue stick with a jerk, turned, and resumed her shooter's stance.

"I want to finish my game."

Cash bristled at the rebuff. He grabbed her by the arm, throwing her roughly against the wall and sending the cue flying from her hand to the floor, where it described a half circle as it rolled to a halt. Jack felt it was his duty to object, having been taught about a lady's honor—chivalry and all—and he stepped between Cash and the girl. Cash evaluated him from slouch hat to scuffed brogans, then chuckled.

"Looky, Gunter, we got us a Reb plow-pusher here wants to take up for the saloon tramp."

"You best go play with the rest of the white trash, boy, so I won't have to hurt you."

As his face reddened at the insult, Jack's long arm swooped around in an overhand arc and landed squarely on Cash's chin, knocking him onto the green felt plane of the billiard table and sending balls careening and bouncing like hailstones off a flat rock. More surprised than hurt, Cash stood down from the table, rubbing his chin and smiling.

"*Oooee.* We got us a real Texas hero here, looks like. You come on outside with me, scarecrow, and let's see how bad you really are."

Jack hesitated, then shuffled after the heftier man's broad back. He did not figure he could whip McCabe, but he darn sure wouldn't back off. Not with that girl watching. As they made their way through the crowded room, some of the locals fell in step, sensing that something that might be worth watching or betting on was about to happen.

When Jack pushed his way through the door after being

jostled about by the fast-forming crowd, Cash was already waiting for him in the middle of the dusty street, squared off with his feet spread. Jack slid sideways between two tethered horses and stopped, facing his opponent. He made fists of his hands and assumed a brave stance. Cash grinned at him and shook his head.

"A grown man doesn't fight with his hands, boy. Where's your weapon?"

Jack was astounded. The man was actually intending to fight it out with guns over a petty misunderstanding. He looked around him at the expectant faces of the press of onlookers, then into the narrowed eyes of Cash McCabe, where he saw the specter of death. He shook his head.

"This is crazy, Mister McCabe. You surely aren't serious. I'm not going to shoot at nobody over a little thing like that in there. I don't even own a gun."

Cash's face darkened. He motioned Gunter toward Jack.

"Give him your pistol, Gunter. Strap it on him."

The albino unbuckled his gunbelt and walked behind the quaking farm boy. He reached around Jack's slender waist and buckled the rig in place. Jack looked down at the gun on his hip and shook his head again.

"No. I'm not going to fight. Not this way."

Before he had finished speaking, Cash drew and fired, taking a notch out of Jack's left ear. Blood streamed down his neck and into his collar. A nervous quiet descended on the gathering in the street. Cash slipped the smoking .45 back into its holster.

"Changed the shape of your ear with that one, boy. I'll make you a new eye with the next."

As Cash moved to draw again, Jack went for the gun on his hip and fired, barely aware how the pistol had come to be in his hand. Through the haze of gunsmoke, he saw Cash McCabe lifted backward off his feet and deposited in the dirt, blood covering his shirtfront in a growing stain. Jack stood transfixed, staring at the smoking weapon in his hand, as the other McCabes rushed in a body to their fallen sibling.

A wave of fear and nausea rushed over Jack as he dropped the gleaming pistol back into the tooled leather pocket of the gunbelt. He spun around and ran to his horse. With a desperate yank, he pulled free the reins and leapt aboard the rangy gelding, then thundered away toward the dark, forbidding prairie, pursued by the angry shouts of the McCabes.

Chapter Two

An anxious examination of his backtrail netted Jack
Dancer nothing but the sight of empty miles of parched
prairie. He had spent the entire day Sunday in random,
wandering flight, wading his horse through creek beds and
guiding it furtively across rocky expanses. He had read in
the penny dreadfuls that desperados often eluded pursuers
that way, and he was a fugitive from justice now. He expected to be overtaken at any moment by a posse of red-
eyed, outraged citizens who would drag him kicking and
fighting to the nearest tree with a sturdy limb. He felt sure
that he had killed Cash McCabe. All that blood.

Would folks take into account the fact that he had attempted to avoid the confrontation with the late Mister
McCabe? Not likely. The McCabes were rich and powerful
men; Jack was only a poor farm boy. He dare not even go
home. His ma would screw up her face in that familiar
expression of disgust and disapproval and accuse him of
being where he hadn't ought to have been, and she would
be right. It was small consolation that he had been backed
into a corner, with only one way out, save being carried

out by the handles. Now Jack was running, with nowhere to go, no one to whom he could turn.

As he topped out on a rise, Jack intently searched again across the empty plain toward Buffalo Springs. Where were they? The McCabes were not the sort to let a thing like this go unavenged. They would come, and they would come to kill. He spurred the gray into a run.

After a time, Old Gray began to falter. Jack pulled back on the reins and slowed the horse to a trot, then a walk. Finally he stopped and dismounted. He looked at the rangy, fifteen-year-old gelding standing spraddle-legged, wheezing and blowing, head down and heavily lathered. He could push the game horse no further. This was no country in which to be afoot. He slumped onto a flat sandstone rock, forearms on his knees, looking over his backtrail. He pulled the floppy-brimmed hat off his head and hung it over the hole in the knee of his overalls, wiping his sunburned brow with the arm of the long johns that hung below his shirt-sleeve. Jack's unkempt mop of blond hair hung in sweaty, tangled ropes over his grit-reddened eyes. He was bone tired and jackrabbit scared. The muscles in his throat bunched in a tight, painful knot and his eyes welled with tears. Dadgum it. Why had he not stayed home?

A hawk soaring directly above him cut loose with one of those shuddering shrieks that go right down to a man's socks. Jack jumped, the piercing cry bringing his thoughts back to the present situation. He watched as a few torn rags of clouds in the western sky ripened from red to purple while the sinking sun sought a place to bed down for the night. He looked around him and spied a tight grove of post oak peeping over the next swell. He checked his back-trail again. Still no sign of pursuit. He took the gelding's reins in hand and walked toward the trees.

Jack led Old Gray into the center of the oak thicket and tied the spent mount loosely to a low bush, then slid the saddle off its back. He laid the saddle carefully on its side, like his Uncle John had taught him to do. He dropped to the ground and lay back wearily. Jack sat up again, only now aware that Gunter McCabe's gunbelt still encircled his waist. He unbuckled the belt and slipped the hateful weapon into a saddlebag, then lay down again. His stomach was chasing his backbone and it occurred to him that he had not eaten all day; there was no food. When he left the farm for a spree in town, he had not planned for a trip across half of Texas. Besides, he wanted to sleep more than he wanted to eat. He had not slept the previous night, and he sought to escape the gnawing thoughts that kept buzzing around in his mind like flies on a manure pile. He wriggled around on the acorn-encrusted turf, grunting and making himself as comfortable as possible. Jack finally drifted into a fitful sleep filled with dreams that were peppered by distant gunfire and peopled by faceless, howling mobs.

Jack awakened to the sound of tin pans clattering and the smell of bacon frying.

He opened red-rimmed eyes to be confronted by the tangled canopy of branches above him. Jack wondered at first why he was not at home in his own bed, then recollection flooded in on him and returned the cold ball of fear to the pit of his stomach. An insistent breeze brought a fresh scent of food that drew him erect as firmly as a rope might, and he crawled to the edge of the trees to peer into the predawn shadows. A chuck wagon was parked invitingly on the flat below, a cookfire winking like a saucy siren as trailhands crossed back and forth across the camp. A quarter-mile further back, he could make out the bedded-down forms of a large herd of cattle.

Jack walked over and bent to pick up the saddle blanket, shooing a pair of daddy longlegs spiders and a cantankerous scorpion from the folds, then saddled Old Gray. He brushed his clothes and smoothed his hair with his fingers, then donned his hat and led the horse from the trees. He gave the prairie toward Buffalo Springs a cursory examination, mounted up, and started down the slope toward the cow camp, his mouth watering.

As Jack neared the ring of cowhands hunkered over their plates, all heads turned to note his arrival. What they saw was a trail-beat farm boy, his ill-fitting wardrobe dirty, disheveled, and threadbare, his face caked with dirt and streaked by sweat and tears, mounted on a tired old horse that had seen better days, but not lately. Most turned back to their breakfasts.

Jack stopped at the edge of camp and sat the gelding, waiting for an invitation to step down. It came from a handsome older man in a black leather vest, sitting on the far side of the fire with one knee up, balancing a plate.

"Light down for some breakfast beans, boy. You look all in."

Jack alit quickly, dropping the reins to the ground. Then he pulled himself erect and tried to appear less anxious. The camp cook, a rather seedy-looking gent with dingy gray hair to his shoulders and sporting a grizzled gray beard, handed him a plate heaped with beans, with a half-dozen thick strips of bacon and a couple of sourdough biscuits piled on top. Jack grasped the plate like it was lost treasure newly found, muttered a "thanks" as he received a spoon from the cook, and wound down to a sitting position, crossing his legs as he descended. He waded in, shoveling beans and stuffing biscuits. He looked up to see the man in the vest regarding him as he ate. Jack slowed his intake then, smiling and blushing a mite.

His mouth full of beans, Jack asked, "Could you men use another hand?"

The man, who he figured to be the trail boss, looked at

the boy intently, taking in his appearance first, but then concentrating on what he could see in Jack's eyes.

"You know cattle, do you, son?"

"No, sir, I don't. As you can see, I'm a farmer. But I'm willing to learn and to work hard."

"Are you any sort of hand with a horse?"

Jack brightened and replied smartly. "Yes, sir."

A surly-looking cowhand got up and dusted the seat of his britches, then walked over and looked down at Jack. The man's nose wrinkled up like he smelled something bad.

"We ain't talkin' mules and plow horses here, hayseed." The cowboy turned his attention to the trail boss. "Shoot fire, Major, look at him. Look at them seedy clothes. Don't even fit him. I won't have him along. He's nothin' but a dumb sodbuster, and a poor specimen at that."

The Major colored a bit, but his reply was calm, if curt.

"I was a dumb sodbuster, too, Harvey, when I was about this man's age."

Jack jumped in then, explaining that for the last three autumns he had helped his Uncle John to capture and break mustangs in West Texas and New Mexico. The Major nodded and pointed with his spoon at a wiry young Mexican standing at the chuck wagon eating his breakfast off the gate.

"Spanish, there, is our wrangler, and he's laid up with boils. Can't sit a saddle. If you figure you can handle a sixty-horse remuda until he's able to ride again, I'll take you on. That will free one of the other hands to help watch the herd. Then, we'll see. Might be we can teach you enough you'll make us a hand to trail's end."

Jack sat up straight, wiped his mouth with his sleeve, and grinned broadly.

"Yes, sir! Thank you."

The cowhand named Harvey turned from the tub where he had just deposited his plate, his face clouded.

"I got a herd to move, Major, and I won't be saddled with a dumb plowboy."

The trail boss pointed at the big man with a steady finger.

"I do the hiring and firing around here, Harvey, or did you forget that? You are my ramrod, nothing more. If this arrangement doesn't sit with you, you can be the wrangler and I'll get another top hand."

"Keep him under your thumb, then," Harvey snapped back, "and out of my way."

Harvey Biggs whirled on his heel, leapt to his pony, and thundered through the camp, nearly bowling Jack over and causing him to spill his plate. The trail cook picked the tin plate off the ground, wiped it on his apron, refilled it and handed it to Jack. The other cowhands all got to their feet and filed by the tub of dishwater to deposit their plates, then they mounted and rode out to take their assigned positions with the herd. The trail boss lingered.

"If Harvey bothers you, you tell me or Swampy, here," he said, indicating the cook. "Now, I'll need to know your name."

Jack hesitated for only a moment.

"Dancer, sir. Jack Dancer."

"You mentioned an Uncle John. Would that by any chance be John Dancer, the West Texas gunman?"

"He ain't a gunman, sir, he's a horse hunter that's handy with a shootin' iron."

Major Amos Warfield smiled and clapped Jack on the shoulder.

"Let Swampy have a look at that ear. Then Spanish can fill you in on your duties." He turned and walked to his horse.

Jack was rounding up the last of the beans on his plate with a crust of biscuit when Swampy grabbed it from his hand and dumped it in the tub with the others. The crusty cook nodded to the Mexican boy, who walked gingerly over to the tub and dove in with a rag. Swampy went to the chuck wagon and unlocked a storage box attached to the right side of the bed, reached in, and withdrew a bottle of whiskey. Then he stepped to the back of the wagon, reached into the *possible* drawer and came out with a handful of bandages and a clean rag. He told Jack to sit down on a rock by the tailgate, then, using the rag dampened with whiskey, began to wipe the dirt and caked blood from Jack's damaged ear. Jack flinched as the rotgut cut through the dirt and the blood to reach the raw wound, but he did not cry out.

"What bit you, son?" asked the scraggly old cook.

"Caught it while crawling through a fence," Jack lied.

"Mmm. Yeah, that .45 caliber bobwire is a booger."

Jack spun his head around and faced a wide, snaggle-toothed grin. He grinned back.

"The Major seems like a fine man."

Swampy was wrapping the ear in bandage. "Yep, he's plumb straight, Major Warfield is. Can be stern, even hard, but he's a fair man, and if he tells you a thing, you can go to the bank with it. He's a rancher now, but he's a man with the bark on. Been a Indian fighter, and he was a officer in Hood's Texas Brigade. Ain't feared of nothin' I know of, 'cept maybe failure."

"Was he really ever a farmer like he said?"

"Naw, I doubt it. He was just sayin' that to bait ol' Harvey."

Swampy tied the final knot in the bandage, shoved Jack's hat back onto his head, and patted him on the rump as a signal to stand up.

"You stay clear of Harvey 'til he cools down a mite. He don't take to bein' brought up short, and since he can't take it out on the Major, he's apt to light into you.

"Now git on out of here so's I can get packed up and

movin'. Them boys will be runnin' that herd right up my backside."

Grace Dancer was a wisp of a woman, standing a shade over five feet. She struggled to heft a bag of flour that weighed half what she did, boosting it higher into her arms with the bump of a knee. She did a little shuffle with her feet to balance her load, then tilted the top and let the white powder pour into the tilt-out bin under the cabinet.

Grace had been an attractive woman once, but her beauty lay forgotten now beneath the rugged ridges of a face carved by time and toil. The faint lines of humor at the corners of her eyes went unused and unheeded, having yielded to the furrows of bitterness that weighted down the corners of thin, rigidly set lips. Her mouth was a harsh slash in her thin face. The yellow-gray hair lying thin and lusterless against her scalp was pulled back severely into a tight bun at the base of her neck.

As the last of the flour trickled from the mouth of the sack, Grace dropped a tin scoop in on top and pushed the bin shut. Taking a pair of shears from a hook on the wall, she cut the sack into rectangular pieces of a size to serve as dish towels, then carried them out to an enclosed porch where she deposited them atop a pile of laundry on the floor beside a wooden tub. A worn, hard-used washboard was leaned against the side of the tub, and several misshapen cakes of lye soap stood in a row on a low shelf against the wall.

Grace was worried about her son, Jack. He had not returned from town Saturday night, or all day Sunday. Jack had been out late a few times, even stayed away overnight on one occasion, but he had never been absent this long. She was afraid he had gotten himself into serious difficulty, but there was little to be done until the trouble made itself known.

She glanced out the door to see a group of riders, suspended inside a thick cloud of red dust, approaching from the direction of town. Reaching calmly around the corner of the kitchen door frame, Grace came out with a shotgun in her hand. She broke it open to check the load, then snapped it shut again and stepped through the screen door into the yard to await the visitors.

The horsemen galloped heedlessly onto the hardpack of the farmyard, sending their dust before them and scattering a squawking flock of chickens in a frantic, feather-flapping flurry to escape the pounding hooves of the horses. The riders halted before the tiny figure brandishing the big shotgun. Grace recognized the McCabe brothers, all four of them, and Carter Bozeman, a weasel of a man in a derby hat with a tarnished star pinned to his vest. Bozeman was the McCabe-appointed, McCabe-paid marshal of the McCabe town of Buffalo Springs.

From the corner of her eye, Grace spied her eldest son, Tom, halt the mule pulling the plow, take the knotted reins from around his neck, and hurry across the clodded rows of the field toward the house. The empty right sleeve of his work shirt flapped in rhythm to each long stride and he held his slouch hat to his head with his left hand. Grace defiantly eyed the angry faces of the mounted men. She stuck out her lower lip to send a blast of air chasing an errant tendril of gray hair that had fallen over her left eye.

"How'd you heathens care to do over the wash on that line your dirt has ruint?"

"Where's your boy?"

The gruff query came from Oran, the oldest of the McCabe boys. He was a brute of a man. Six-four, two-sixty, with a full black beard that was turning white around his mouth. His cold gray eyes were small and set close together, almost hidden beneath a protruding simian brow

of coarse black hair that stretched over both eyes. It occurred to Grace that the man had no neck, no neck at all.

"Good morning to you too, Oran McCabe. If you mean
Little Jack, I got no idee where he is. He went into town
Saturday night and ain't come home as yet."

The tall, lean-muscled, one-armed farmer rushed up to
side the woman. His steady brown eyes carried the question
from one mounted man to the next, but he asked it of his
mother.

"What's going on, Ma?"

"Where's your brother, Tom?" Oran asked. "He shot
Cash and took out runnin'. We want him."

"Told you he wasn't here," Grace said.

"Hope you ain't doubtin' my ma's word, Oran." Tom
looked at Cash, noting the bandaged shoulder and the un-
characteristic pallor of the younger McCabe's skin. "What
do you mean, *shot* Cash? . . . Jack don't even own a gun."

"I give him mine," Gunter said, "and he run off with it."

A slight smile played on Tom's lips.

"Gunter, you ought to know better than to give a Dancer
a gun and stand a Yankee in front of him."

The intruders stiffened in their saddles as if on signal
and menace was common in their eyes.

"We'll be back to teach that boy his place," Oran said
as he reined his horse around. He spurred his mount
roughly and trotted from the yard, his brothers peeling off
in turn to follow. Marshal Bozeman lingered. He shifted
the tobacco wad that bulged his cheek from one side to the
other and spat at a chicken, sending it squawking across
the yard.

"I'll expect you to turn Jack to me when he comes home,
Tom."

"You and I both know that you expect only what the
McCabes tell you to expect, Carter. Jack will come in, all
right, but only to return Gunter's weapon. It's evident what

happened here. Now get off my place 'fore I throw you off."

The marshal's hand moved to his pistol, but the barrels of Grace's shotgun stared him down. With an indignant snort he showed them his back, slapped his horse on the rump, and rushed to catch the others.

Chapter Three

Jack had been correct about one thing: the McCabes were not the sort to let any wrong done them, any slight, real or imagined, go unavenged.

In 1867, armed with a carpetbag full of Yankee dollars and a head full of schemes for plunder, Dad McCabe had come to Texas, following the passage of the Reconstruction Act by a radical Republican Congress that insisted a "hard peace" be foisted upon the Confederacy. Texas was on its face, under a strutting military regime, its coffers bare, its towns, countryside, and frontier at the mercy of bands of carpetbaggers, ruffians, displaced Negroes, and rampaging Indians. General Charles Griffin had been installed as one of five district military commanders in the South, and when Democratic governor Throckmorton of Texas opposed the repressive practices of the occupation forces, he was stripped of his office and replaced by Unionist E. M. Pease. The smugly hostile and totally corrupt administration was rife with fraud and excess. Federally appointed judges and tax assessors, openly seeking personal riches, consorted with bloodsucking profiteers like McCabe to pick the pockets of the defeated South. Under the guise of legal procedure, land, crops, and assets were seized for nonpayment of impossibly inflated taxes and sold at government auction for a fraction of their worth. There had been no authority to which the conquered could appeal. The Texas Rangers, upon whose vigilant protection so many frontier families had depended during the war, had been disbanded and replaced by newly formed State Police units manned by toughs and criminals. With shiny new government-sanctioned badges on their swelled chests, the swaggering men of these units were commonly known to abuse their authority, even to the extent of larceny, rape, and murder. Wherever men resisted the unfair and oppressive practices, federal troops were called in to enforce the radical misrule. Those who did not comply were driven from their homes to become exiles and outlaws. Chaos and confusion reigned as the dreams of native Texans ended afloat in a glass of raw whiskey and branch water.

Finally, in 1873, Texas was returned to the control of Texans. But by that time, McCabe had made his fortune and held sway over a vast and powerful financial empire encompassing cattle, land, and commercial enterprises. The Boston native and his sons continued to wield that power with a heavy hand, imposing their wills upon their neighbors with ruthless abandon, tolerating no trespass upon their domain or upon their actions.

The old man had been livid when advised of the shooting in Buffalo Springs. He had been less concerned with the wounding of his son than he had been about the wounding of the McCabe pride. Dad McCabe maintained his position of power through force and intimidation, and he knew that it was imperative that the illusion of McCabe invincibility be preserved. For one of his sons to be bested by a penniless bumpkin that did not even own his own weapon, who had to borrow the bullet from another of his sons, almost sent the old man into convulsions. With a face showing the high purple of rage, his eyes bulging from deep sockets, he issued an edict to his progeny to exact suitable McCabe justice upon Jack Dancer, and to do so before any of the young hardscrabble farmer's peers might be inspired to stand against the family's might.

Cash McCabe sat on the spacious porch of the three-story, twenty-room, seven-gabled house atop the highest knoll in the county, his feet propped on the rail, holding a near-empty bottle of sourmash on his lap with his good arm. He was seething with bitter hatred and humiliation.

Cash was a young man filled with himself, exceedingly proud of his gun skills. The ivory grip of the nickel-plated Walker Colt he wore about his waist was proudly etched with five notches, each denoting a man who had fallen to the fury of his gun. The burning pain of the wound in his shoulder was a constant, throbbing reminder of his own carefree behavior and lack of vigilance on that Saturday night. He had toyed with the boy, baiting him to amuse and impress his brothers and the other spectators. He should have put a bullet in Dancer's heart straightway. Why, that farmer might even have killed him! You don't give any man, woman, or child an even break if they have a gun to bring to bear against you. He knew that, but had ignored it while enjoying his natural superiority and his mastery of the moment. It was not a mistake he would make again. The flesh wound in his arm would soon heal. Then young Jack Dancer would die—and it would not be an easy death. The boy would pay dearly for the ragging Cash's brothers had given him, and for the censure he had been forced to endure from the old man.

Cash tilted the bottle to his mouth and drained the last of the sippin' whiskey. He flipped the bottle off the porch in a high arc, drew, and fired. The bottle exploded into a powdery cloud of shattered glass, the particles catching the rays of the sun to form a sinister spectrum of color.

An anticipatory smile settled on McCabe's face.

"Next one's for you, Jack Dancer. I'll dump what's left of you in that old woman's lap."

Little dew had formed during the night and the rich buffalo grass was relatively dry, so the Major passed the word that the herd would not move out at dawn as usual, but would be allowed to graze for a couple of hours while the crew drifted them north. By the time the men began to throw the cattle on the trail by closing in on the broad drift of bawling, half-wild range animals and squeezing them into a ragged line of march, shouting "Ho, cows, ho, ho," Spanish had Jack filled in on his responsibilities as wrangler.

Wrangler was the lowliest job on any drive, and not the easiest. Tending and driving the remuda of remount horses would be Jack's main chore—having fresh horses ready for the cowhands as they were needed, steering the horse herd clear of any dangers of the trail, keeping the spirited animals away from the herd of cattle. He would regularly check hooves for damage, inspect legs, haunches and withers for energy-sapping parasites, doctor cuts and sores, and haze the remuda to night camp and into a rope corral, ready for the next day's work. On top of that, the wrangler doubled as a clean-up and errand boy for the cook. Jack figured it to be a full-time job.

Spanish was a shy, quiet young man, only a couple years older than Jack was. His real name was Luis Antonio Cordero, and he was the youngest in a family of fourteen children. His father, a *vaquero* in Old Mexico, had hoisted baby Luis onto a saddle before the child took his first step. Spanish had been on his own since the age of twelve, working the ranches of the Gulf Coast. He was a small man, slender and whip-like, his complexion darker than many Negroes Jack had seen. He had a mouth too full of long

yellow teeth and wore a slender mustache on his upper lip.
Jack liked him.

Spanish told Jack that the 2500-head herd originated near
Victoria in southern Texas, and was destined for southeast
Wyoming, a drive of 1200 miles that would take four
months to complete. This was a seed herd, brood stock for
the Major's ranch, south and east of Cheyenne.

Jack Dancer proved to be as good as his word, handling
the skittish cowponies of the remuda with ease and skill.
Jack was work-hardened by long hours of toil in the fields
on the farm, but he was unused to working in the saddle.
By the time the sun was overhead, his thighs and rump
were raw and screaming. Each jogging stride of his mount
sent ragged red bolts of fire through his stiffening body,
and he gritted his teeth against the pain. Only stubborn
pride, and the knowing grin on Harvey Biggs hard features,
kept him in the saddle. Jack kept wishing the sun toward
the horizon, but the torturous day dragged on and on, last-
ing the longest fifteen hours he had ever known.

At days end, Jack limped into camp looking like death,
wishing to heaven he had let Cash McCabe kill him.
Swampy spotted the agony on his face and grabbed him by
the sleeve, leading him around the end of the chuck wagon
and away from the amused eyes of the other hands. The
cook fetched a can of salve from the possible drawer, then
ordered Jack to drop his pants.

"You'll have to peel off them long johns, too," Swampy
told him.

Standing as naked as the day he was born, Jack reluctantly allowed the cook to spread the cool, soothing salve
over his raw, chafed flesh, fighting to keep the tears from
his eyes. When he had done, Swampy gestured for him to
climb back into his clothes and told him to come around
and get himself some grub. The other cowhands grinned

and chuckled among themselves as Jack took the plate of beans over into the shadows, eating on his knees.

Swampy fixed Jack up with a bedroll from the extra gear in the chuck wagon, and as he was flopping around trying to get comfortable, one of the cowboys came ambling over to him.

"Howdy. I'm Long Bill Jakes. These here is an extra pair. Use 'em if you can."

Jakes tossed a roll of clothing in front of Jack's nose, turned and walked back toward the fire. Jack unrolled the bundle. It was a pair of wool pants with buckskin sewn over the seat and down the inner thighs. There was also a worn vest and a faded bandana inside. Jack muttered a weak thanks after the tall man's retreating back, looking at the cowboy like he was Santa Claus.

It took the displaced farmhand the better part of a week to become inured to being all day in the saddle, but Jack never voiced a complaint or tried to weasel out of a job, and by the time Spanish was healed enough to resume his duties as wrangler, Jack had been accepted by the other hands—except for the ramrod, Harvey Biggs.

Major Warfield turned Jack over to the care of a young colored cowboy they called Smoke.

"Ride with him 'til you get the hang of it all. Smoke's as good a hand as I've got. Do what he tells you, when he tells you, and you'll learn. If you think you can't handle the job, you're better off to head for home now, for we can't afford to keep a man that isn't able to haul his own weight."

"I'll handle it."

The men had taken to calling him Plowboy. Jack resented it at first, thinking they were making sport of him, but he said nothing, and after a few days he began to answer automatically to the alias. That night at supper, he asked Smoke about it, noting that most of the trailhands had colorful nicknames. Grinning, Smoke explained that it was a common practice in the profession, and that the names were a sign of acceptance by one's trailmates, and often a badge of honor.

"Some is obvious, like for me, Smoke . . . and Spanish. And Long Bill, Curly, and Cotton don't take a lot of figurin'. Copperhead there, his name's really Charlie Grissom. Got no more fear of snakes than a chaparral cock. He be ridin' along the middle of nowhere, he sees a snake, he gets down and grabs the slithery booger, whirls it around and 'round, pops off its head. Gives some of them to Swampy to cook up, but I don't eat none of it."

Jack saw then that Copperhead wore a rattler's skin as a hatband and that his belt was fashioned from the skin of a big diamondback.

"What about Swampy? That ain't his real name, neither."

"No," Smoke told him, "real name's Will Masters. Always awash in whiskey. He runs out, he gets as mean as one of them snakes."

"I've never seen him drunk," Jack said.

"Maybe not, but you never seen him really sober yet, neither."

Smoke paused to wipe the last of his food from his plate with a crust of biscuit, downing it with a smack of his lips. He set the empty plate on the ground at his feet and pulled the makin's from a vest pocket, offering the tobacco pouch and rolling papers to Jack. Jack refused with a wave of his hand. As he rolled a cigarette, Smoke went on to explain that Cap, John Wentworth, was an ex-sailor, and that French Tom Cady was from Louisiana and spoke the language that furnished his moniker.

"Some says he had to leave out of N'Orleans in a hurry. Supposed to have killed some big politic fella in one of them duels."

"How 'bout Harvey? He doesn't get called nothin' else."

"Harvey, he's just too mean to stand still for any name that'd fit him, and nobody likes him well enough to bother, nohow. He sure give you yours, though, that first night. . . . *Plowboy*. You steer clear of Harvey. He's mean, even for a white boy."

In the rambling conversation with Smoke, Jack learned that the cowboys to be found on the great trail drives were indeed a diverse lot. One in six was Mexican. One in six was Negro, most of them having been slaves or the sons of slaves on Texas ranches where they had been taught the skills of roping and riding. A few were Indians or breeds. After the war, mustered-out Union soldiers and disillusioned Rebel veterans had taken to the range, but that had been almost a generation ago now, and they were mostly gone. The seedy-looking cowhand sitting next to you, eating his beans off a tin plate, might be a moneyed patrician or a penniless immigrant peasant from Europe. Bizarre English remittance men, drifters, rangeland beggars, saddle bums, and bumpkins like Jack Dancer—all could be found on the long trails to Kansas, Wyoming and Montana. There were men on the dodge from the law with untraceable aliases, and former lawmen tired of putting their lives on the line for forty a month. In cattle country, you did not ask about a man's past. The average age of a cowboy was twenty-four, and Smoke explained that after a few years of chousing mossyhorns, most men got jobs in a town, in a store or some such, either because they had gotten stove up or tied to a skirt.

"What about you, Smoke? How'd you get into this line of work?"

"Born to it. My daddy was a slave on a ranch near Galveston, but Mister Fletcher, he never treated him as such. Daddy's a top hand, and after the war he stayed on. I was just a sprat then, and I been working cows long as I can recollect.

"My real name is Joshua Cooper, but I ain't heard it in so long, I'd likely pay it no mind."

"That don't bother you, bein' called Smoke?"

"Naw. I been called a site worse."

Jack did not know how to reply to that, so he said nothing.

"Once you learn what you got to know to ride herd on your own, Plowboy, you best not take your meals with me. The white cowboys generally stay separate from the coloreds and greasers."

"I've never needed nobody to pick my friends 'til yet. See no need to change."

The day the Indians came, Jack was still riding with Smoke, learning his trade. They had pushed the herd across the Red out of Texas and into The Nations on the day after Jack joined the drive, crossing at the rough border village of Red River Station, the easiest ford. Now the drive was seventy miles into Indian territory, and these were the first red men the drovers had seen. There were four of them, sitting on their ponies atop a knoll to the west, silhouetted by a dazzling afternoon sun at their backs. Somewhere ahead, the trail boss signaled for a halt. Jack and Smoke were at swing position, and they received the signal to hold up from Cotton Beckwith, riding point. Smoke passed it along to Curly Beale on flank, who in turn signaled the drag riders. The mass of milling cattle slowly ground to a halt, like some gigantic piece of machinery winding down.

The Major had beckoned to Cotton from his position ahead of the herd and now, having received some special instruction, Cotton was coming back this way at a run. He paused as he rode by to tell Smoke and Jack that the trail boss wanted Spanish up ahead in case the Indians could not speak English. As Spanish rode forward, Jack fell in beside him, ignoring Smoke's admonitions to stay where he was.

As the two cowboys neared the chuck wagon where the Major stood talking to Swampy, the Indians headed their ponies down the slope. When Spanish rode on up to the wagon, Jack held back a few yards. The Major glowered at him, but said nothing.

"Hao."

The tall Indian raised his arm in peaceful greeting, stopping ten yards out from the line of white men. His pony was positioned slightly in front of those of his companions. He was an old man, frightfully thin, his skin hanging like draped fabric over hard, cordlike muscles in arms and shoulders. Old battle scars stood out like white, gnarled ropes on the bronze background of his bare torso. A buffalo headdress sat like a crown on a head of winter-white hair that hung in braids to his waist. His only weapon was a lance, the gleaming point held proudly aloft.

"Howdy." The Major returned his greeting. "You speak English, there, Chief?"

The old man looked right and left at the faces of his copper-skinned companions for signs of understanding, receiving only guttural grunts and blank looks for his effort. The horses of the Indian party pranced nervously in place, churning the red dirt under their hooves. The trail boss tilted his head at his wrangler and motioned toward the feathered visitors indicating that Spanish should try his hand. The young *vaquero* was a bit cowed at the spectacle of the naked aborigines on their spotted ponies. He swallowed once, then timidly advanced, removing his sombrero and holding it over his heart as if in the presence of a primitive deity.

"Habla usted Español?"

No reaction.

"*Hao,* Bear Paw."

The greeting came from behind Spanish and The Major. Jack Dancer walked his horse forward, grinning broadly. The Indian stared at the young white man that had called him by name. The light of recognition sparkled in the lively old eyes and his stoic face was transformed by a wide, toothless smile.

"*Hao,* Little Jack. I did not know you. You have become a man." Bear Paw spoke the words of greeting in the Kiowa tongue, then continued. "We come to you, my young friend, skulking like coyotes, leaving our pride in our lodges. My people are starving. The government agent cheats us. He sells the cattle sent to the Kiowa by the White Father and puts the money in his pocket.

"The long knives have long ago taken our guns and our young men cannot hunt. They have lost their skills with the old weapons. The buffalo have fled before the white man's cattle, and papooses cry with swollen bellies in the lodges of the Kiowa.

"I come to the white man to beg like a Digger Indian. I ask only for a few of your cattle so that my people might have meat in their cookpots. I do not ask for myself or for my braves, but for the women and children."

Jack struggled to keep his voice from cracking as he relayed the Kiowa's pitiful request to the Major. The trail boss did not reply for a moment, but stood looking at Jack in wonder. Then he issued orders to Cotton to cut out a half-dozen head.

Harvey had ridden up in time to hear Jack translate the Indian's words.

"You ain't going to give these snivelin' redskins our beeves, are you Major? Let the thievin' savages eat buffalo chips for all we care."

"Get away from here, Harvey," The Major said sharply. Harvey threw his hat to the ground in a tantrum, then, seeing the fiery glare in the trail boss's eyes, turned and stomped away, screaming back over his shoulder.

"Your call, but ain't none of it comin' out of my pay!"

The Major turned back to Jack. "Can you talk that gibberish as well as understand it?"

Jack nodded. "Some."

"Then tell . . . Bear Paw, is it? Well, tell him that we give him this unworthy gift of six poor cattle. The Kiowa are our friends, and friends are not beggars. Ask if he will accept these few animals, though we know they are inferior to the great buffalo. He will honor us to accept our humble offering. And . . ."

The Major turned to Swampy, who handed him two cloth sacks, one of sugar and one of flour.

". . . ask if he will take these to his women, to do with as they will."

Jack relayed the Major's message in halting Kiowa, adding on his own an apology for the behavior of Harvey Biggs. Bear Paw nodded solemnly. A look of dignity had been restored to his wrinkled features. The Indians turned their ponies. Two of the younger braves broke off to receive the cattle that had been cut out of the herd for them.

When the Kiowas had gone, Major Warfield told Swampy and Cotton that they may as well make camp here since it was getting on toward evening and the herd was stopped anyway. Then the trail boss motioned for Jack to follow him and they sat together on the grass at the foot of the slope.

"Where'd you learn that Kiowa lingo?"

"My Uncle John, sir. He's done some horse trading with the Kiowa and the Cherokee. He stayed with us one winter and taught me to talk a little bit of both tongues. Figgered it might come in handy sometime."

"Well, it sure enough did today. Thanks, boy."

Jack smiled and nodded.

"And Mister Dancer . . ."

"Yes, sir?"

"Don't ever do that again. If I want you in on something, I'll let you know."

Chapter Four

The Major had been alerted to a band of hoodlum trail cutters working the Chisholm between the Washita and Canadian Rivers, so he issued the order for all hands to go armed. Some of the men already wore belt guns—French Tom, Long Bill, and, of course, Harvey Biggs. Swampy kept a double-barreled Greener ten-gauge behind the spring seat of the chuck wagon, and the boss carried both a side-arm and a Henry rifle in a saddle scabbard. The working cowboys did not carry long guns on their saddles for the practical reason that the protruding stocks could easily snag their reins or lariats.

After a supper of sonofagun stew and sourdough biscuits, a welcome change from the more typical fare of beans and salt pork, the men who did not own their own weapons lined up at the front of the wagon to be issued arms from spares the cook kept locked in the tool box. Copperhead had his own gun, a Colt Peacemaker that he kept with his other valuables, and the other men took their picks from Swampy's offerings. Jack sat at the fire, nursing his coffee.

Smoke walked over, a mouthful of white teeth shining out of his dark face as he proudly adjusted the belt and slid

the old Pond-made Smith & Wesson in and out of the holster.

"Better get on over there, Plowboy, 'fore they all picked
over."

Jack hesitated, then slowly unwound and crossed to the
wagon where he kept his saddlebags. He dug inside and
retrieved Gunter McCabe's shiny, new Beaumont-Adams
.44 five-shot pistol and the ornate holster. After a moment's
hesitation, he slipped it around his waist. For a moment,
the night in Buffalo Springs flashed vividly into his mind's
eye—his nose filled again with the acrid odor of powder
smoke, and he heard once more the sound of a bullet thud-
ding into human flesh as somewhere a girl screamed. That
old knot of fear balled up in his stomach. He squeezed his
eyes shut and took a deep breath. After a moment the memory dissipated, wafting away into the night sky with the
smoke from the camp.

When Jack walked back to the fire he was greeted by a
chorus of envious "ooos," "ahhs," and low whistles, which
turned his face as red as the dying embers at the edges of
the cookfire. Harvey Biggs walked over to regard the fancy
rig hanging on the farm boy's spare frame.

"Now how the hell did a nothin' plowboy come by a
fancy iron like that?"

"I took it off an albino Yankee with a smart mouth,"
Jack said.

The gathered drovers broke into raucous laughter as the
ramrod bristled under Jack's impertinent reply.

"Well then, mister *badman,* since you're totin' such a
fine arsenal, you can just take Smoke's turn at night guard.
We'll all feel a lot safer with you out there to protect us
from Booger-bears."

Jack Dancer had earned his spurs and was now pulling
his turn at the various jobs tending the herd. However, the

ramrod's unexplained animosity toward him resulted in his drawing more than his fair share of riding drag and night herd.

As far back as he could remember, Jack had heard about the glamorous, exciting life of the Texas cowboy, but he had discovered since joining the drive that it was sweaty, dirty, back-breaking, butt-busting labor—no more romantic than staring at a mule's backside while plowing a field. The cowboys themselves perpetuated the myth, considering themselves to be hard-riding, fast-shooting knights of the range, and Jack had to admit that he felt the same manly pride in being accepted as a member in this exclusive club of frontier Lochinvars.

Like all the hands, he disliked riding drag, eating the dust generated by ten thousand plodding hooves for sixteen hours at a stretch, but he found he rather enjoyed the equally-dreaded job of night herder, at ease in the cool stillness of the dark hours amidst the small noises of the bedded-down cattle. The crooning calls of the other night guard from across the heads of the herd blended with the choral chirpings of crickets and the marathon serenades of whippoorwills and mockingbirds. He waved at Long Bill Jakes as they passed in their opposing orbits around the sleeping cattle, and as he heard Long Bill's singsong rendition of "My mother had a wooden leg, my sister's chest was cedar ..." he thought that he was not much of a balladeer. That was another myth that had been exploded for Jack. Smoke had a fine voice, and Jack enjoyed listening to his rich tones as he sang the spiritual work dirges of his heritage. Curly was a passable singer, often opting to play a soothing tune on his old-mouth organ. But most of the others, like Jack himself, were not very musical. They did not so much *sing* while they rode as *recite* in a low, rhythmic chant. It did not seem to matter much to the cows, the whole purpose of it being to not startle the skittish animals and set them to running. One just sang out, to let the easily-alarmed beasts know it was a man out there riding around, not some hungry, long-toothed, sharp-clawed predator looking to put beef on its menu.

Three furtive shapes moving noiselessly through the dark shadows of the tall grama grass to the east of the resting cattle went undetected by Jack Dancer as he rounded the head of the dormant herd in the opposite direction. The Comanche braves waited until both night herders had faded from sight, then sprang to their feet, waving wolf pelts in the wind and letting the fearful odor of the killer beast carry to the herd. The chilling howls of a wolf pack closing for the kill split the silence as the Indians raised their chins to the sky. As of one mind, the cattle were on their feet and running in an earth-trembling, frightened mass—an unstoppable sea of trampling hooves and ripping, clattering horns. Jack's seasoned cowpony reacted more swiftly than he did, lunging into a full run away from the charging tempest of terror-stricken longhorns that thundered down upon man and horse.

Jack bent low on the horse's neck, his heart pounding in his throat, as he eased his mount toward the outskirts of the stampeding mass of cattle. Behind him, over the roar of thrashing hooves, he could hear the shouts and whoops of the other men as they joined in to contain the spread of the herd's flight. Shots rang out in the din like the muffled sounds of corn popping. Lather and spittle from the laboring horse beneath him slapped Jack in the face, burning his eyes and blinding him.

The pony finally pulled away from the hurtling shapes at its heels. The death that rode the wild, broad backs of panicked beasts thundered past. Suddenly the ground disappeared beneath the flashing hooves of Jack's screaming mount. Jack hit the ground with shuddering impact. He rolled to a stop and pushed himself up on his elbows, turning just in time to see the sky blotted out by a huge black form that came hurtling in on top of him. Then everything ceased for the dethroned night rider as he was carried away into the smothering, crushing arms of oblivion.

Jack did not know how long he had been unconscious, but the sounds of the stampede and the shouts of the men had faded away. He heard the pulling and chomping sounds of his horse cropping grass on the level above him. He tried to move, activating the twelve-hundred pound longhorn cow that pinned him to the rocky bed of the dry wash in which he lay. The cow thrashed about, bawling piteously, unable to rise on its broken front legs, grinding and crushing Jack beneath it.

Jack lay still, fighting for breath. A small cry of agony left his lips to be carried harmlessly away on the persistent breeze that traveled the course of the gully, the wind bearing a woeful moan of its own.

He heard the creak of saddle leather from above.

"Help . . . down here!"

The murky form of a rider appeared at the lip of the wash. Jack strained his eyes to make out who it was, but the man's hat cast his face in a dark shadow. The face opened in a smile, exposing a toothy crescent of white against the gray backdrop of his jaw. The rider laughed, and a shudder of fear shook the young man held captive in the wash.

"Harvey? Harvey . . . help me. I can't move."

The ramrod leaned down from the saddle to pluck Jack's hat off the edge of the embankment. Then he walked his mount over to the grazing cowpony to grab hold of the trailing reins. He looked down again at Jack Dancer, helplessly pinned beneath the crippled cow, then turned away, laughing as he rode from sight.

When Harvey Biggs rode into camp, he picked his way through the prone, deep-breathing bodies of the disheveled,

exhausted cowboys. He stopped his horse in front of Major
Warfield and dropped something at his feet. The flickering
light of the fire reflected off Jack Dancer's battered hat.

"That's all's left of your precious plowboy."

The Major looked up into his ramrod's smirking face.

"Did you ever figure out who your daddy was, Harvey?

Jack awoke to the distant rumbling of thunder from the
southwest. He had slept last night, off and on, waking when
the cow that pinned him jerked about in pain. The poor
beast was still alive, its breathing shallow and labored. The
thrashing about it had done during the night had moved its
heavy body around some, so that now it rested only on
Jack's legs, still holding him captive but giving him a bit
more freedom of movement. Jack tried to free himself by
pulling from under the longhorn's crushing weight, by
pushing against its back, by digging in under his own legs,
all to no good purpose. A sudden, brilliant flash of lightning
directly overhead was followed instantly by a deafening
boom. Jack and the cow jerked in unison, startled by the
fierceness of nature's wrath. It began to sprinkle, and it
occurred to the hopelessly-restricted youth that a heavy rain
could soon fill the dry wash with a torrent of water. For
the first time, he realized that he might die there.

"Think, Jack, think."

Recalling the injured animal's reaction to the clap of
thunder, Jack twisted around until he could reach his pistol.
Flipping off the rawhide loop that secured the .44 in its
holster, he drew the weapon, braced himself upright with
his left arm and laid the gun beside the cow's ear. He pulled
the trigger.

With a raging bellow of fright and pain, the longhorn
flopped and twisted as Jack scampered from beneath its
bulk. He pulled himself away from the cow and fell back,
catching his breath, allowing his pulse to slow and the pain

in his battered body to subside. Then he struggled painfully
to his feet. A grunt of pain escaped his lips. Every muscle
in his body seemed bruised. He limped over to the groaning
cow and aimed the pistol at its brain, pulled the trigger,
and put an end to its agony.

It started to rain. Jack clambered from the gully and
limped off up the trail, following the herd.

When he thought back on it later, he would consider it
the most brash and reckless thing he had ever done, but
Jack Dancer was fighting mad and he waded in with no
regard to the possible consequences of his actions.

Following a trail of smoke and the smell of cooking meat
Jack came upon a Comanche village of a half-dozen or
more hide teepees, protected from the elements in a shallow
canyon surrounded by a thick wood of blackjack trees. He
surveyed the camp from under cover. He spotted a cowhide
stretched on a frame of willow branches, leaning against a
rock. A group of ragged Indians were gathered around a
cookfire, gnawing ravenously on chunks of singed beef,
blood running down their chins and onto their chests and
shirtfronts. Filthy, gaunt children sat in the dirt, their bellies
distended, their cheeks plump with white man's beef.

Filled with a growing fury, Jack fished a cartridge from
his pocket and reloaded the empty chamber in the cylinder
of the .44 pistol clenched in his fist. He holstered the sidearm and burst into the Comanche camp, striding purposefully toward the cluster of staring, incredulous savages. One
startled brave stood and walked to intercept the white in-
truder. He raised an arm in tenuous greeting.

"Hao."

Jack launched into a diatribe in the Kiowa tongue, knowing the Comanche were close cousins to the Kiowa and
would understand him well.

"You stampeded the cattle of my people, causing us great

harm. You came in the night like coyotes, to steal from men you feared to face in the light of day. If you had asked, we would have given you cattle, as we gave cattle to our friends, the Kiowa. I would deny no man food when he is hungry, even a Comanche. If you have honor, you will pay for what you have stolen. Give me a horse and you may keep the cattle."

The Comanche chief stood before him with feet spread, anger clouding his face. Jack tensed, ready to go for his gun. Then, remarkably, the brave's face relaxed and he laughed.

"You have the heart of a warrior, young one. You shall have your horse."

He signaled to a young Comanche of twelve or thirteen and the boy disappeared behind the lodges. He returned in a few minutes, leading a pony with a blanket across its back. He handed the rope halter to the brave, who transferred it to Jack's hand.

"Are you hungry, white man?"

Jack was, but he figured he had pressed his luck far enough.

"No, thank you. I must go."

"Then go in peace," the Indian said, "but do not return. If you come again to my village, I will kill you."

Jack mounted and rode slowly from the compound, the hair bristling on the back of his neck. The Indian stood watching after him until he disappeared into the trees, a smug smile playing on his face. The horse he had given the young white man was the cattle drovers' own, a stray picked up after the stampede.

Tom Dancer was weary as he led the mule into the barn. He had spent the whole day getting that danged oak stump out of the near corner of the north pasture where he wanted to build the pig sty. It was a thing that had to be done, for that corner was the only spot on the place with shade enough for the hog pen.

He hung the harness on a nail in the stall post, then fumbled with the lantern, holding it against his body with his stub. He struck a match, clutching it between his index and middle fingers, forced the globe up with his thumb, then crooked his fingers to bring the flame to the frayed tip of the wick. It flared to life as the globe slipped off his thumb and slammed down on his fingers.

"Drat."

The yellow light chased the gloom into the corners as he set the lantern on an upended crate. Then he stooped to pick up a gunny sack with which to rub down the mule.

His arm was bothering him this evening. Not the one he still had, the one he had left at the battle of Pea Ridge. After all these years he still got pains in his missing fingers, hand, and elbow. Phantom pain, some called it. Felt real enough to him.

Tom did not often dwell upon his disability. A man made do with what he had. Had it not been for his Uncle John, a man two years his junior, he would not be alive at all. They had joined up together, fought together all through the war. When he had fallen at Pea Ridge, it was John that dragged him from the battlefield as Yankees with fixed bayonets darted around them on all sides, overrunning their position. The battle had been lost, as had the war. Fool war, anyhow, fought for reasons that had nothing to do with poor Texas farm folk like the Dancers.

When he had recovered from the amputation of his arm and gotten out of the hospital in Van Buren, Arkansas, the war was over. He had come home to find his ma with a newborn baby in her arms and his pa dead, murdered by a drunken hider on the streets of Fort Worth. John had stayed on with them for three years, helping Tom run the farm and caring for his sister-in-law and his nephew, Little Jack.

Little Jack. Where in tarnation had that boy got to? Tom had raised him, acting more as a father than a brother, and he worried some about him now. Not as much as Ma, for Tom knew that Jack had more to him than Ma gave him credit for, but he missed the boy, and he could surely use his help around the farm. He figured Jack had run off thinking he had killed Cash McCabe, and he hoped that wherever his brother was, he would get the word and come on home.

The tantalizing aroma of chicken frying made its way from the kitchen to the barn, sneaked past the smells of hay, mule muffins, old leather and sweat, to set Tom's mouth watering. He sped up his grooming of the mule.

There were no trees to hide their approach, so the McCabe brothers stopped their horses in a deep erosion ditch a hundred yards west of the farmhouse. It was coming on dusk and they could see a light shining in the barn. Oran and Avery stayed in the gully to cover them as Cash and Gunter skittered across the yard in a crouched run, pistols drawn. They ducked under the window, flattened themselves against the gray, weathered front of the barn, and Cash sneaked a peek around the frame of the open door. Tom was inside, grooming a grizzled, old jenny mule. Cash crept across the threshold on tiptoe, Gunter close behind him. Cash cast his eyes around the interior, holstered his gun, and reached to take a trace chain off a hook by the door. He advanced slowly and quietly toward the farmer's broad back, the sound of his approach covered by Tom's hearty, off-key humming of "Onward, Christian Soldiers."

Cash swung the chain high overhead and brought it down with vicious force against the back of his victim's head. Tom dropped like he had been boned.

Cash stood, teeth clenched, reliving the humiliation of being bested with a six-gun held in the shaking fist of a boy in brogans.

"Give this message to your little brother, clod-kicker."

He moved in and brought the heavy chain down again on the fallen man's head and back. The mule screamed, kicking its heels in the air, and bolted to the end of its tether.

The harsh, frantic braying of the mule brought Grace Dancer bounding from the house with a shotgun in her hands as Cash and Gunter McCabe dashed from the barn. She raised the gun and pulled back both hammers as Oran McCabe fired from the ditch behind her. The tiny woman flew forward as the rifle bullet struck her, lifting her frail frame off the ground, then slamming it to the hard clay surface. Triggered by her fall, twin blasts from the shotgun sent a rain of pellets into the barn door that erupted into a cloud of wood dust and splinters, leaving a hole the size of a washtub.

Gunter McCabe, cowering on the hardpack in front of the barn, yelled and slapped at his face as his cheek bristled out with splinters, like a bleached-out barrel cactus.

"I been shot! I been shot!"

As Oran and Avery rushed up, Cash was scrambling to his feet, whacking at the dust on the seat of his pants. Gunter was screaming.

"Quit your hollerin', you bloodless freak," Oran shouted. "You ain't shot, you're punctuated."

Avery came wandering from the barn, shaking his head as if in a daze. He had seen the brutally bludgeoned body of Tom Dancer. Now he stood staring down at the motionless, bleeding form of Grace Dancer. His face matched his brother Gunter's colorless cast.

"A woman. Oran, you overgrowed idiot, you gunned down a woman."

"So? Would you druther I'd let her blow Cash and Gunter in two?"

"Yeah, but a woman. What are we going to do?" Avery

was terrified. "Killing Tom is bad enough, but the old lady . . ."

Oran looked around, then pointed to the barn.

"Drag her in there with that one-winged farmer. We'll fire the barn. Nobody will ever know but what they both run in there and got trapped."

"Hold off, there," Cash said. "I want folks to know what happens when you mess with a McCabe!"

Oran looked at his youngest brother as if his brain was pudding.

"You stupid hothead. They string a man up by the thumbs for mussing a woman's lip rouge in this country. Drag her in there . . . *now!*"

Cash and Avery each grabbed an arm to pull the limp form of Grace Dancer into the barn. They deposited her unceremoniously on the straw-strewn earthen floor beside the body of her son. Cash picked up the lantern from the crate where his victim had placed it and tossed it overhand into the loft where hay was stored. They stood a moment, watching, waiting for the hay to catch. A loud *whump* was followed by a white ball of flame as the coal oil from the shattered lantern ignited. They ran into the yard, pushed shut the damaged door, and dropped the bar in place, then followed the disappearing figures of Oran and Gunter, running hell-bent for leather saddles.

Chapter Five

The discordant, foghorn-bellowing of the mule cut through a haze of unconsciousness and pain to bring Grace Dancer back into tortured reality. Fiery brands showered down from the blazing loft in an evil rain of destruction as the panicked jenny dashed around the barn's interior seeking escape. Billows of noxious smoke sucked the air from her lungs as Grace pushed herself to a sitting position. She cried out when she spied the blood-drenched body beside her, then collapsed again in a fit of coughing. Her hand traveled to her own bloodied side where the rifle bullet had torn her flesh.

Avoiding the flying hooves of the mule as it bounded past, she struggled to her feet and clambered to the door in a three-pointed stance. She pushed against the unyielding door. Grace bent down and scrambled through the hole made by the double load of buckshot, ripping a bloody groove in her back as she fell into the yard.

Gulping the air like a quaking drunk inhaling the first beer of the day, she lay quivering a moment, then forced herself once more to her feet. The night sky glowed with a deadly orange cast and the soaring flames from the roof bathed the yard in dancing patches of light and shadows. The tiny woman hefted the heavy bar from its nest and let it fall to the ground, then flung wide the door. The braying mule bolted past in a blast of searing air and dashed into the night, trailing streamers of smoke from patches of burning hair on its back.

Grace forced herself back into the inferno, holding low to the ground. Peering through smoke-generated tears, she made her way to the body of her son. She grabbed the blood-soaked collar of his shirt. As she gripped it, red liquid oozed between her fingers. With a strength she did not normally possess, the frail woman dragged the heavy, precious burden inch by inch from the disintegrating building, into the yard, and away from the roaring flames and blistering heat.

Grace Dancer fell in an unconscious heap across the body of her son, completely emptied of energy and resolve. At that moment, the barn collapsed, sending fiery columns of glowing embers and brands swirling into the black sky of the Texas plain.

The herd was bedded down on the north bank of the Canadian River when Jack caught up to the drive. He could make out the glow of a fire beyond the silhouetted mounds of the resting longhorn herd.

The river was up, the current swift. The pony he had acquired from the Comanche balked as he eased it toward the brown waters, so Jack explained his intentions with a sharp jab of his spurs that sent the horse plunging into the stream, swimming strongly. The men were hunkered around the fire when he rode into camp.

"Plowboy!"

The trailhands rushed in a body to greet him, but he slid off the side of his horse and hit the ground running, straight for Harvey Biggs.

The startled ramrod jumped up, dumping his plate from his lap, as Jack Dancer dove the last four feet, driving his shoulder into Harvey's midsection. Both men went tumbling, and both jumped quickly to their feet. Harvey swung a wicked roundhouse blow that Jack ducked under as he smashed both hands into the other man's ribs. Harvey grabbed him by the shirt and vest, swung him around and slammed him into the unforgiving trunk of a cottonwood tree. Jack slid to the ground, landing spraddle-legged, and Harvey followed with a driving right to the cheek that stunned the younger man. Harvey backed off as Jack struggled to his feet, then drove a meaty fist into his stomach that took the young man's wind. Jack pedaled backward, gasping for air, then rushed in swinging with both fists, catching Harvey with a straight right that bloodied the big man's nose and sent him into a rage.

Slavering and charging like a rutting stag, the ramrod caught Jack with a looping left that knocked him staggering and followed it up with a clubbing right that drove him to his knees. Jack came up fast, hooking to the body. Harvey swept Jack's arms aside and hammered him with a vicious flurry of rights and lefts that backed him across the camp. Then he grabbed Jack's collar with both hands and brought his head down to collide with a rising knee. Jack's nose broke with an audible *pop,* spattering both fighters with blood. The battered youth wilted to the ground, landing on his face.

Jack tried to rise and fell again into the dirt. Harvey half-turned to walk away, a derisive sneer on his lips. Jack lurched forward to wrap his arms around the ramrod's knees, too weak to inflict any damage, but unwilling to break off the battle. Harvey made a club of his fists and brought them sweeping down on the back of Jack's neck, driving him once more to the ground. He withdrew, a look of confused concern on his face, to watch the young cowboy writhing in the dirt.

Smoke and Long Bill rushed to their fallen friend and helped him to a sitting position.

"Stay down, Plowboy. That's enough."

Jack looked up into the concerned faces of his trailmates. His nose and eyes were beginning to swell, his lips and cheeks were cut and bleeding. He struggled to his feet, pushed the supporting arms of the two cowboys aside, and staggered toward the ramrod in an erratic path.

The fire of battle in Harvey's eyes dimmed and retreated, inexplicably replaced by a cold look of dread.

"He's crazy!" Harvey backed away and drew his gun. "Keep him away from me or I'll have to put him down!"

Swampy raised the heavy spoon he held in his hand above his head and whacked Harvey's gun hand, sending the pistol skidding across the trampled grass and scuffed earth of the campsite.

"Grab him. Hold him off." The Major issued the order, sending Smoke, Long Bill and Cap to restrain Jack Dancer. "And Harvey, you get out of here and cool off."

Harvey bent to retrieve his weapon, then hurried to his horse and leapt into the saddle. "I'll be back when you got that whelp hobbled and tied." He rode from camp, muttering wildly to himself.

As Harvey melded into the thickening dusk, the men released Jack's arms. Smoke led him to a spot near the fire and lowered him to a sitting position. Swampy stuck a tin cup of steaming black coffee under his nose. Major Warfield moved to look down upon his resurrected, but battered, trailhand.

"What the hell was that all about, Jack?"

Jack dropped his head between his knees to spit a stringy puddle of blood between the heels of his brogans. He knew he had gotten the hell beat out of him, but, inexplicably, he felt a surge of triumph.

"Harvey knows."

Swampy's bellowing voice intruded into the predawn darkness to rouse the men from their blankets.

"Off your rumps and on your stumps, or I'll feed this mess to the coyotes."

Jack groaned and rolled over. His head was throbbing. He sat up and tried to open his eyes. Both were swollen shut. For a moment he thought he had gone blind and panic sent a hand to his face. The puffy typography of his features made evident his affliction. Lumps, knots, cuts and scrapes, all painful to the touch, had transformed his face into something resembling the hoof-churned mud at the bottom of a catch corral.

Using a thumb and an index finger, Jack pried open one eye. He was staring at the Major's boots. The trail boss chuckled.

"Swampy, put this man in the chuck wagon today. See if you can fix him up enough his mama will know him when he gets home."

Jack rode on his back in the wagon; jostled like dice in a cup and subjected to the nonstop dialogue of the camp cook. The herders had killed a cow that broke a leg in the stampede, so Swampy put a chunk of bloody beef over each puffed eye and tied a bandanna around his patient's ears to keep the meat poultice in place. He had swabbed him down with liniment and salve, too, and the redolent fumes of the medications hung like a fog inside the canvas confines of the chuck wagon. Jack complained throughout the plodding twelve-mile trek to night camp, but his protestations skipped off the chattering cook's ears like a flat rock on still water.

By the time the wagon halted and Swampy was opening

the chuck box and kindling a fire for supper, one of Jack's eyes was open and he could see through a narrow slit out of the other. That night, over a mountainous mound of beef and beans, he related to the rest of the crew, as they leaned forward in rapt attention, what had happened to him since the stampede. He told them about the crippled cow that had held him prisoner under its pinning bulk and of his nervous foray into the Comanche camp.

"When that big ol' Indian handed me the reins on that pony, I thanked him and lit out, figurin' I'd worn my welcome thin."

"Don't that beat all," Smoke said, grinning ear to ear as he shook his head in wonder. "Plowboy, you got more grit than a Texas sandstorm, but I sure got some doubts as to where you left your smarts."

Jack nodded in agreement, smiling crookedly with puffed lips, wincing at the pain the action caused.

"If I'd thought longer, I'd of circled wide of the Comanch' for sure, and just hoofed it back here."

But when questioned again about his attack on Harvey Biggs, Jack's only response was, "He knows." The ramrod was conspicuously absent at the fire that night.

Swampy, Jack, and Smoke sat sipping the last of the coffee, watching the dying embers of the fire as the other hands peeled off one by one to go to their blankets.

"By the way, what happened to my hat?" Jack asked.

"We buried it," Smoke said.

"*Buried* it? What in tarnation did you do that for?"

"Man, we thought you was dead. Ol' Harvey said he figgered the wolves had dragged off your carcass. Your hat was all we had of you to bury."

"Come and get 'er, boys. A special treat today . . . beans for breakfast."

Swampy's raspy call brought a chorus of groans from

the blanketed mounds of waking drovers in the camp. Jack forced open a swollen eye to see Spanish busy at the chuck wagon, breaking out the plates and spoons. Tossing the cover from his shoulder, he forced himself to a sitting position, then resignedly arose from his night bed to roll his blanket.

As the hands queued up to be served, Harvey Biggs was first in line, a privilege of the ramrod. Jack stepped out from the others and walked up behind him. He plucked the high-crowned hat from Harvey's head and placed it on his own. It fell to his ears, so he took it off, removed the bandanna from his neck and worked it around under the sweatband. When he planted it again atop the ash blond mop of unruly hair on his head, it fit like the skin on a peach.

Harvey glared at Jack with hatred smoldering in his eyes. Followed by the stifled snickering of the crew, he walked away, bareheaded, an unendurable state for any cowboy.

The days that followed were as uneventful as could be expected on any trail drive. They endured one storm that pelted them with hailstones the size of quail eggs. The faces of the cowboys were covered by welts where the merciless missiles of ice had struck them, lending them all, for a time, the same battered expression that Jack wore as a result of his fight with Harvey. The driving hail storm stampeded the remuda, and when the panicked ponies were brought under control, several were missing.

The drive was stopped several more times by parties of gaunt Indians begging for beef, and in each instance Major Warfield rewarded their humble entreaties with a gift of a few head of cattle.

When they had choused the last bawling longhorn across their final crossing of the Cimmaron, out of Indian Territory and onto Kansas soil, the men put away their six-guns and steeled themselves for the grueling hundred-mile push over a waterless grassland to the Arkansas, near Dodge City.

The prairie they traveled was dotted with the wagons of ragged bone-pickers collecting the sun-bleached, chalky remnants of the buffalo slaughter of the early '70's. These gypsy scavengers roamed the plains, collecting the randomly strewn bones of the great woolly beasts that, a generation before, had populated the prairies in herds numbering in the millions. The buffalo had been the sole source of food, shelter, clothing and trade goods for the proud nomadic tribes of Indians that once ruled the savage kingdom of the plains. Swampy told Jack that the bone-pickers sold their ghoulish gather to the manufacturers of a wide variety of goods, from fertilizer to bone china.

Harvey Biggs no longer took his meals with the rest of the drovers. He would carry his plate far from camp, to eat his meal and to escape the glowering scrutiny of the man they called Plowboy.

The long, dry drive began to tell on the parched cattle. The animals became restless and hard to govern. The cowboys were kept on the run, pushing individual cows or small groups of the half-wild longhorns back into the flow of the herd as they broke off in wild attempts to turn back to the last waterhole they could remember. The drovers were forced to change mounts often, for the extra running in the relentless Kansas sun soon tired the little cowponies.

Fearing another stampede, Major Warfield ordered an accelerated drive, figuring it better to have each animal trot off a few pounds in the forced march than to risk losing a good portion of his herd. The faster pace was hard on the men and the animals, but it was proven effective when, four days later, the cattle caught the scent of the Arkansas River over the next rise and broke into a pounding, bawling run for the water. Jack imagined he even saw smiles on the faces of the contented longhorns, standing belly deep in the cool liquid.

Since it had been decided that they would hold the cattle at the river for a few days to allow them to rest and graze, the trailhands were expectant when the Major called them together at the gate of the chuck wagon. The false-fronted saloons, stores, restaurants, and bawdy houses of Dodge City lay just across the river and over the next prairie swell, and every man was hopeful of some time in town.

The Major took a handful of greenback dollars from a black cashbox and stood stoically before his fidgety crew. They were as bedraggled and trailbeat a lot as he had ever looked upon, but he knew his words would put life in their eyes and a spring in their steps as nothing else could do.

"Men, I am advancing each of you a portion of your pay. Dodge City is just over yonder, and I reckoned some of you might want to mosey over that way while we are stopped here. A store-bought bath wouldn't do any of you any harm. I won't tell you what you can or cannot do in town, but I am telling you to stay out of jail. We've a long trail yet to travel and I need every man of you."

The trail boss doled out the wages, then stood watching in amused wonder as shirttails and horse's rumps disappeared in a cloud of dust over the rise. The optimistic cries of young men on the prowl for pleasure drifted back to camp.

"Yahoo!"

"Heeyaw!"

"Dodge City, here I come."

"Whoop, whoop, whoop!"

Chapter Six

Long Bill, Jack, and Smoke hurried from the livery toward the boardwalks, their heads swiveling to take in the sights and sounds of the bustling cowtown that was Dodge City.

"Me and Smoke are headed for the bathhouse and a hot tub, Long Bill," Jack said, trotting to keep pace with the stride of the taller man, "then I am going to find a barber and get me a store-bought haircut. Never had one. Watched it done, though, and figure to give it a try."

Long Bill held back.

"You two go ahead on. I've forded so many dadgum rivers and cricks these past two months, I may never bathe again, if the tub ain't full of whiskey. Besides, them deflowered doves over at Kelley's don't give a whit what a man smells like if his money's the right color."

The two cowboys soaked their trail-beat bones the better part of an hour, Jack got his store-bought haircut, then, shining like new dollars and smelling of toilet water, they made their way to a general mercantile. Jack intended to buy himself some proper clothes for the trail and Smoke had promised himself a new belt knife.

A bouncing bell at the top of the jamb announced their entry. Jack held the door as a large woman with an armful of packages swept past, dragging a tow-headed kid with a snotty nose and a pole of horehound candy stuck in his face. They hit the boardwalk without a backward glance. Jack pushed the door shut behind them.

"Welcome, ma'am," he said.

The store was one large room with shelves to the high ceilings on two walls. Countertops, shelves, and walls were crowded with merchandise of every imaginable sort, and the floor was filled with stacks and barrels of goods. Saddles, horsecollars, harnesses. Pickles and crackers in barrels, shelves lined with canned goods, sacks of flour, coffee beans, salt, and sugar. Glass jars filled with peppermint sticks, sour balls, and horehound candy. Bolt upon bolt of bright-colored cloth, racks of suits and coats with sheepskin collars, shirts and pants in folded piles. Jewelry, shotguns and rifles, ax handles, baby dolls, tobacco, harmonicas. The mingled odors of all these treasures created an aroma that Jack could not get enough of, and he inhaled deeply.

"Be right with you gentlemen."

A timid-looking gnome of a man in a bow tie, black galluses, and white shirt under a dust-smudged apron was grinding coffee beans behind a counter. He was wearing thick-lensed spectacles that lent him a toad-like stare and he had a tiny mustache under his nose that resembled a caterpillar. The young trailhands looked at one another and grinned.

"He's cute as a spaniel pup," Jack whispered.

The comment spawned a giggle from behind the cupped palm Smoke held over his mouth.

While Smoke bent over a glass case that displayed a wide assortment of knives, scissors, ladies' fancy combs, shaving mugs, and mustache cups, Jack surveyed the ready-made clothes on the shelves at the back wall. He selected a pair of blue denim pants and a collarless cotton shirt the color of a robin's egg, roomy enough to allow for shrinkage. He picked up a four-X beaver hat and set it on his head, lifted it up and down, then set it aside. He unstacked the pile until he found one a quarter-inch larger in size, and settled it in place above his brow. A pair of brown, pointed-toe boots of tooled leather rounded out his shopping spree.

The clerk walked around to face him across the counter.

"Got somewhere I can change?"

The little storekeeper pointed him to a back room behind a curtained door, then stepped across the room to wait on Smoke.

When Jack pushed the curtain aside and walked back into the store he was grinning ear to ear, holding his old clothes in a roll under his arm. The sharp creases across the knees of his pants and down the front of his shirt served to certify the crisp newness of the garments.

He paid the clerk for his purchases, then asked, "Mister, can you post a letter for me?"

"Be my pleasure, sir. I'll get you some materials."

The little fellow toddled to a roll-top desk abutting the back wall, and gathered a fistful of supplies. He then offered Jack a blank envelope, pencil, and a sheet of writing paper. Jack addressed the envelope to his brother, Tom, then handed the pencil and paper back to the storekeep. He transferred enough of his advance wages to his pocket for a few glasses of beer, then slipped a sheaf of paper money inside the envelope. He licked the flap shut.

The diminutive clerk wrapped Jack's old clothes in brown paper and tied the bundle securely with string off a big spindle on the counter. Smoke had found several knives he fancied, but it was a big decision, and he wanted to think on it a while. They headed for the door and for a few beers with their friends.

"Come back the next time you're in Dodge."

The storekeeper's statement was punctuated by the jingling of the bell and the closing of the door.

Smoke saw him before Jack did. As his smile faded, he
threw out an arm to halt his friend. Harvey Biggs stood in
the street, his feet spread, his body tilted forward in anticipation. He was teetering slightly from the rye whiskey he
had thrown down at the mahogany bar in the Longbranch.
His fingers were spread wide and working, his right hand
poised an inch above the black, gutta-percha grips of his
six-shooter.

Jack's eyes were drawn past Harvey's shoulder to a
dumpy woman in a red satin dress trimmed in black ostrich
plumes, watching from the open door of the saloon. Her
melon breasts struggled to escape the low cut of her gown.
He thought her figure looked like a busted bale of hay.

"Plowboy!" Harvey's shout commanded Jack's attention.

Smoke pulled at Jack's sleeve, trying to coax him along
the boardwalk and away from the impending trouble. Jack
pried the dark hand free and placed his bundle in it, then
stepped off the boardwalk into the dust of the street.

His mind raced back to a street in Buffalo Springs, and
to the woes his last gun trouble had brought down upon
his shoulders. Jack had no plans to further compound that
mistake.

"This is as far as you're going with this outfit, hayseed,"
Harvey yelled. "You can fork your horse and head south
for Texas . . . *now* . . . or you can face my gun."

Placing one booted foot in front of the other, Jack Dancer
began to inch his way toward his antagonist, talking as he
came.

"I'm not drawing on you, Harvey . . . and I'm not leaving."

He stopped close enough to Harvey's face to see the
beads of perspiration forming on the ramrod's brow and

the bridge of his nose. Jack slapped him, hard, across the face.

Jack started walking forward, his work-hardened palms steadily slapping Harvey's head from side to side in painful rhythm, backing him across the rutted street. The backs of Harvey's legs struck the side of a horse trough and Jack placed an open palm on his chest.

"Cool off."

A gentle shove of his hand sent Harvey plunging backward into the trough, dispatching a sheet of water onto the street and splattering the boots of three men who stood watching.

Harvey came up sputtering and flailing his arms. Jack had turned and was walking back toward Smoke as Harvey climbed from the water. A madness that surpassed rage filled the ramrod's eyes as he went for his gun.

"Plowboy, look out!" Smoke screamed the warning, knowing it was too late.

Jack whirled, slapping leather as twin reports from opposing six-guns careened off the false storefronts of Dodge City. Harvey left his feet, landing again in the trough. The hole in his chest dispensed a liberal red stream that tinted the water a deadly shade of pink.

All heads turned in the direction of the smoking barrel of a six-gun in the steady hand of a ruggedly handsome man in his late thirties. The gunman was rigged out in the trailworn clothes of a working cowhand, but the impression he made was of something much more deadly.

The stranger leathered his gun and walked over to Jack. "That may not have been the bravest thing I've ever seen, boy, walking up to that hombre that way . . . but it was damn sure the most stupid." Jack stared at the man for a moment in numbed surprise. Then he grasped him by the shoulders.

"Uncle John! What are you doing here?"

"Waiting for you."

Jack and John Dancer sat at a table in the Dodge House over coffee. Jack was slumped back in his chair, a blank expression on his face, his eyes glassed over with tears.

"Ma . . . how is she?"

"She'll be alright, but your brother Tom is in bad shape. He's never come around after the beating he took. The doc don't know if he'll live or not."

"Did they catch them . . . the McCabes?"

John shook his head. "Nobody tried very hard, boy. You know Carter Bozeman and where his loyalties lie. Old Dad McCabe's got him in his pocket. Says he looked for 'em, but that's a damn lie.

"They'd left the country by the time I'd got wind of it and got back there, and I hadn't the time to find out much more than that. Had to catch up to you 'fore you got plumb to Wyoming.

"Dad McCabe was talking it around that it was self-defense, trying to use his influence to smooth things over and buy his boys off the hook. But ain't nobody swallowin' that. They shot a woman, and that don't hold in Texas!"

Jack sighed deeply and pushed his chair back from the table. He stood up and turned to leave.

"Whoa. Where you figger you're goin'?"

"Home."

"Just simmer down, Little Jack. That ain't the way, runnin' off in a fret. You showed a cool head out there in the street, even if your judgment did come up a little short of the good sense God give a goose.

"We'll go, but we'll go together and do it right. You ride on out there to your herd and explain to that trail boss how come you've got to quit the drive. Then come on back here.

We'll have us some supper and get a good night's rest. Leave fresh in the morning."

"Sorry about Harvey, Major."

The trail boss shrugged and gripped Jack's shoulder.

"Plowboy, somebody would've had to shoot Harvey Biggs sooner or later. Might even have been me."

"Hate to leave you shorthanded, sir, and I'm mighty grateful for all you've done for me, but this is a thing I have to do."

"We won't be caught short. I'm making Long Bill the new ramrod, and there'll be no problem picking up a couple good hands in Dodge.

"Shucks, boy. There's real cowboys in these trail towns. I won't be forced to take on any farm boys that are greener than August persimmons." He was smiling when he said it. "You've been a good hand, son, and if you ever need work, you come on up to my place in Wyoming. There'll be a spot for you. Good luck."

Major Amos Warfield took Jack's hand in a warm, firm grip, then turned his eyes back to his herd and rode from camp. The rest of the crew gathered around Jack Dancer, shaking his hand, slapping his back, wishing him well. Swampy expressed a special thanks.

"Plowboy, your signing on gave me a rare chance to sharpen my doctorin' skills, I'll say that. You ate your beans without no complaints, boy, and I count that a personal favor. Watch your scalp, hear?"

Long Bill and Smoke lingered after the others had gone.

"Son," Bill said, gripping Jack's hand, "I seen you become a man on this trip. I hope we cross trails on down the line." He stepped into leather, urging his horse to a trot and leaving Plowboy and Smoke alone.

"Smoke, I'm going to miss you. I've learned from you, and I count you as my friend."

Smoke sniffled and rubbed his nose on his sleeve.

"Must be catchin' me a cold," he said. "Plowboy . . . you the only white boy ever looked at me and seen a man. I'm purely sorry you got to leave. Hope we come across one another again sometime."

Jack's throat tightened up on him and he cleared it with a brisk "harumph."

"Goodbye, Joshua Cooper. If you ever have need of anything I got to give, you've only to ask."

Leaving Smoke waving after him, Jack rode to the top of the rise in the trail that led to Dodge. He turned in the saddle and looked back on the sea of hardy longhorn cattle grazing contentedly on the rich grasses, as the bone-tough cowboys he had come to know so well in such a short length of time sat loosely in their saddles, smoking and gazing out across the heads of the herd, looking toward tomorrows on the trail, doing a hard, dangerous job that no breed of man had ever done before them. He had made friends here, good friends. Sharing dangers, bad food, and worse weather as a matter of course and without complaint. There had been many a good time around the embers of a dying campfire at the end of a long, hard day.

He turned his face toward Dodge City and his thoughts toward home.

Jack looked across the table at his uncle and saw the man he had always wanted to be.

John Dancer was a man who knew who he was and what he was about. Bred to the six-gun, bred to the law of strength. He was a known man, a fast gun. Feared by some, respected by many. At thirty-seven, there was a lightening at the temples in the brown of his hair like tempered steel. The lines carved by wind and weather in the rawhide of his face looked deeper than Jack remembered, but the thrum of iron still rang when he spoke and his quick, brown eyes had lost none of their sharpness. The trim mustache on his upper lip served as an adjunct to the strong chin and the granite set of his jaw. His movements were fluid and deliberate. He was a hard man, sure, but a fair man, and strong. Strong in his loyalties. Strong in his convictions.

John looked up from his plate to find Jack studying him. "What's the matter? I got food on my chin or something?"

Jack shook his head, smiling.

"Then finish your breakfast. We got a long trail ahead of us."

They emerged onto the boardwalk into the bright sun of a new day.

As they walked into the livery, the hostler led two saddled mounts through the barn from the corral out back.

"Here you are, Mister Dancer, all ready to go."

The stableman handed over the reins of John's big black, placing the other animal in Jack's care. The horse was a large, young buckskin with a black mane and tail, deep in the chest, rangy, built for long days over miles of dusty trails. Jack's own saddle was cinched onto the gelding's broad back. He looked at his Uncle John with questioning eyes.

"Brought him with me from Texas," John said, while casually checking the rigging on the black. "Knew you took off on Old Gray. Two things a man needs in this country . . . a good gun and a good horse. He's yours."

John Dancer glanced at the shiny pistol riding his nephew's hip.

"We'll do something about that play-pretty once we get to Texas."

Chapter Seven

It is said that even Lucifer avoids August in Texas.

It was midday when they rode through the deserted street of Buffalo Springs. They headed for a forlorn cluster of box-like frame structures perched on the open plain that made up the residential section of the shabby little trail town. The clacking whir of insects from the coarse brown stubble of the fields seemed to add a stifling intensity to the swelling heat.

They had been traveling since long before daylight, a hopeful tactic to avoid the worst hours of the summer sun. The buckskin and the black labored under the weight of their riders, whose shirts were plastered to their backs like blistered paint on an old barn.

The Dancers swung stiffly from their saddles before a squat, unpainted house and tethered their mounts to the pickets of a dilapidated fence enclosing a front yard no bigger than a pair of patchwork quilts. Hard red dirt showed through the yellowed grass in large, round patches, like bald spots on an old man's head. A big red ant hill stood defiantly in the center of the dirt path that led to the porch. To the right of the door, a flower bed had been scratched

in the hard-packed clay, but the faded plantings had sur-
rendered to time and place and lay wilting in the sun. A
rusty hinge emitted a shriek of protest as Jack pulled open
the gate.

The front door was swung wide in hopes of a breeze, so
John opened the screen and they walked into the house.
They picked their way through a labyrinth of loaded
clotheslines to the kitchen. Grace Dancer was hunched over
a washtub. Her elbows rose and fell in a monotonous ca-
dence as she tortured a shirt on the corrugated ribs of a
washboard. A view through the screened kitchen window
saw more lines filled with laundry crisscrossing the back
yard. The house smelled of lye soap and bluing.

"Hi, Ma."

Jack rushed to throw his arms around the sparrow of a
woman. She gave him a cheek for a salutatory peck, but
her manner was cold. She looked him up and down, noting
the new trail clothes, and uttered a *humph* to herself.

"Tom's in there."

Grace indicated a bedroom with a toss of her head. She
gave John Dancer a scrutinizing look that was a mate to
the one she had given her son, then returned to her laundry.

From where the tub stood in her kitchen, Grace could
look out the window through the shimmering haze of heat
to the gabled bulk of the McCabe house in the distance,
looming darkly atop a high hill like some hovering, Gothic
gargoyle. The sight inspired a bitter burst of energy that
was transmitted down her thin arms to her fingers as she
resumed her scrubbing with a vengeance, venting her pent-
up anger on the poor garment in her tightly clenched fists.

Jack opened the door to find Tom sitting slumped in a
ladder-back chair. A shaft of amber light forced its way
through the pulled shade, illuminating his still body. Tom's
blank eyes stared straight ahead. His brow was beaded with
sweat and his chin was covered with drool and slobber.

Jack grasped the back of the chair and scooted his brother out of the sun. He removed the neckerchief from around his throat and wiped the spit from Tom's slack chin.

"Tom. I'm home, Tom."

When Tom showed no reaction, Jack moved to look into his brown eyes and found that his brother no longer lived inside them. He bent and kissed him on the forehead, like a man saying good-bye to a loved one lying in a coffin. He turned and walked from the room.

Jack stopped in front of his mother. "Ma . . . I . . . ." There was nothing he could say.

Grace craned back her neck to look into the eyes of her tall, young son.

"I sold the farm, Little Jack. There's no need for you to stay around here anymore.

"You come along too late in life for me to appreciate you. I didn't want another young'un to tend. I was already tired.

"When Big Jack was killed after Tom went off to that damned war, I reckon I just gave up.

"You've done your best, I suppose, I'll give you that. But there's a wild streak in you, boy . . . like your Uncle John's got. I reckon I just let you run free.

"But what you got into with them McCabes is why my son Tom is sittin' in there in that chair with a head full of mush . . . and I don't want you here no more.

"Tom will die. Sooner the better, then I'll follow after. I wish you well, Little Jack, but I don't never want to look on your face again."

She picked a pile of soiled socks off the floor and dropped them in the wash water, then began to soak and scrub them one at a time. Grace was as much alone in the house as if the others had never existed.

Jack shouldered past his Uncle John with tears streaming down his face. He pushed open the screen door and paused a moment on the porch, but he did not look back. He continued out of the yard to his horse. John followed and they swung into their saddles and walked their horses away.

Neither man spoke as they retraced their steps through Buffalo Springs. As they cleared the edge of town, Jack turned in the saddle and looked at John.

"Where do we start to hunt the McCabes?"

John Dancer urged the black forward and bent to grasp the reins of Jack's mount, halting the buckskin. He moved beside his nephew, placing a gentle hand on the younger man's shoulder.

"Little Jack, I figure Tom would rather you catch back up with that herd. I can handle this chore for the Dancers."

Jack looked him in the eye, frowning. His jaw was tensed and jutted forward.

"I'm going, with or without you." He spurred his horse ahead.

"If you're dead set on doing this thing," John told Jack as he pulled even with him, "I reckon that makes us partners. Can't say as I'll mind the company."

They stopped at every ranch and farmhouse seeking news of the McCabe brothers. They halted wagons on the rutted roads and spoke to farmers in the fields. The Dancers made all the little towns in North Texas, inquiring in the saloons and brothels and jails, but the men they sought had vanished from the area with no traceable sign of their passage. They headed for Fort Worth to outfit themselves for what was shaping up to be a long and grueling quest.

"First thing we're doing when we hit town, Little Jack, is get you a handgun—one that won't send a flash plumb across Texas when the light hits the barrel."

John slipped his own weapon from the holster and handed it across, butt first, for Jack to examine. The pistol was a Colt single-action Army revolver, popularly called "The Peacemaker" or "The Frontier." It was chambered for

.45 caliber, center-fire cartridges and had a seven-inch, blue-black barrel. The grips were walnut. It was a work gun, in perfect condition. The holster on John's looped belt was plain leather. Jack noted the sightless barrel of the Colt. John explained.

"That sight's filed off so's it don't hang up during a hurried draw. Might save your life. If you like that one, we can get you one to match it, or we can get something's not quite so heavy. Don't ever wear a gun that'll attract the attention of every young hothead on the prod, like that one there of Gunter's. A gun is a tool, not some symbol to prove you're a man. When we get you fixed up, I'll teach you to use it."

"One like this would be fine, sir." Jack handed the weapon, butt first, back to his uncle.

"Whoa," John said, settling the Colt in the leather pocket and slipping a rawhide loop over the cocking piece, "I said when we started out we were to be partners. You drop the 'sir'. Makes me sound old, somehow. Just call me John."

"Yes, sir—I mean . . ."

John leaned sideways in the saddle and stared intently at a spot under Jack's nose where he was growing a little puppy mustache. He laughed aloud.

"You let that brush on your upper lip get out of hand, reckon I'll be callin' *you* sir."

Jack smiled, blushing. He did not mind the teasing. It was an indication to Jack that the man cared. He did wish he would refrain from calling him *Little* Jack, though, and he asked John if he might drop the diminutive prefix.

"Reckon not. My brother, your daddy, was Big Jack. You are Little Jack. For a spell yet, anyhow." John smiled like a man with a secret plan.

At a gunsmith's shop in Fort Worth, Jack traded the fancy sidearm and gunbelt for a Colt revolver, brand new, and a used Henry rifle in fine condition. The pistol was a twin to John's gun, except that it was .44 caliber so that the cartridges for his handgun would fit the Henry too.

The horses were tethered in front of the shop. The gunsmith had thrown in a rifle boot to seal the deal and while Jack was strapping the gunbelt of the new Colt around his waist, John fitted the boot to the saddle on the buckskin and nestled in the Henry rifle.

"Let's leave the horses here and walk over and talk to the marshal. Maybe he's heard something."

They crossed the street, dodging horsemen, wagons, and buggies to the marshal's office and entered. The lawman was lean and tall, balding, and a paunch was beginning to show at his belt. His weathered face was pleasant, but alert for trouble. John extended a hand across the desk, which the marshal accepted with a firm grip. Jack followed suit.

"Name's John Dancer, Marshal. This is my nephew Jack."

"I heard of you, Dancer, and I figure I know why you're here. I heard tell of that fracas up at Buffalo Springs. You're lookin' for the McCabe boys?"

John nodded. "Seen 'em?"

The marshal shook his head. He pushed to his feet and circled the desk to a coffee pot atop a dormant potbellied stove. He poured a tin cup full of the rank-smelling brew and offered it to both men, who refused.

"Coffee's cold, but it beats firing up the stove in this weather." He returned to the desk, sipping from the cup as he walked. "No, I ain't seen 'em. Leastwise, not that I know of. Wouldn't know 'em if I did, but I ain't heard nothin', either."

Jack leaned both hands on the lawman's desk.

"You'd know them, sir. One of them is an albino, no color to him."

The marshal leaned forward, showing increased interest.

"You don't say? Heard tell of such, but I never seen one. Anyhow, they must not be in town. I'd surely have heard something that unusual.

"Tell you what I think. If I was on the run, I'd head for the *Llano Estacada*, the Staked Plains. That's a mighty wild part of the country, with a bad crowd. A man could get lost in a sea of wanted faces. I'd start looking in Mobeetie. You look up Temple Houston. He keeps abreast of the goin's on up that way, and that albino feller will stand out like a white kitten in a litter of black pups."

An expression of surprise lit John Dancer's face.

"Temple Houston, you say? He's a friend of mine. Last I heard, he had a law practice down in Brazoria."

"He did 'til a couple of years ago," the marshal told him. "The governor appointed him district attorney for the thirty-fifth judicial district . . . after two others had turned it down on account of it was too dangerous a job. Hired him more for his skill with a six-gun than for his law smarts, but if you're a friend of his, you know he's got both in ample supply."

"Thanks, Marshal. I'll fire a letter off to Temp, let him know we're coming and have him be on the lookout for the McCabes. Appreciate your help."

The marshal rose again from his swivel chair and hitched his belt as the Dancers prepared to leave the office.

"Sorry I couldn't be of more help to you, and I hope you catch up to them no-accounts. But Mister Dancer, I know your reputation with a gun. If you should happen across them ol' boys while you're in Fort Worth, you let me handle it. I don't tolerate no gunplay."

They were camped in a grove of willow trees on the banks of the Wichita. John was working on Jack's gun, filing off the sight. He finished, ran his hand over the end of the barrel, and blew on it to clear it of filings. He tossed the Colt to Jack.

"C'mon. Time you learned to handle that weapon the proper way."

They climbed out of the draw and walked a couple hundred yards from camp so they wouldn't spook the horses. John reclaimed Jack's weapon, slipped it from the holster, emptied the cylinder into his hand, and slipped the cartridges into a vest pocket. Then he buckled the gun belt around Jack's waist, taking particular care how it settled on his slender hips. He pulled and tugged, then stood back, checking how it looked. He pulled and tugged some more.

"That feel comfortable?"

Jack nodded.

"The grip ought to be setting about halfway between your fingers and your elbow. Let your arm go limp."

He lifted Jack's hand and let it fall. He repeated the action several times.

"Now you do it. Let your arm swing against the butt of your gun."

Jack did as he was told. Satisfied that the gun rig was hanging right, John bent down and tied the thong around Jack's leg. It felt to Jack like it had been there forever.

"Now take hold of the gun. Don't draw it out, just take hold of it."

Jack's hand slid onto the smooth butt of the pistol, his fingers curling around it without any conscious thought, then he felt his thumb on the hammer.

"Now pull the gun and point it straight in front of you, right over there."

The gun was out before John finished speaking. Jack had been concentrating on drawing the gun, and there it was, in his hand and pointed.

"Damn." John Dancer looked at his young partner. "You been practicing without my knowing?"

"No."

They worked for over an hour on Jack drawing and aiming the weapon. Then they walked back to camp. They sat down in the shade and John showed him the clicks for safety, half cock, and full cock. He taught him how to break the Colt down, to take it apart and put it together again. Then he had him clean and oil it. John walked to his saddlebags and came back with a can of leather soap. He tossed it to Jack.

"Work that into your holster."

The Dancers would stay the better part of a week in camp, practicing with the guns. John filed away some of the cocking piece so Jack's thumb could snap it into full cock when his hand hit the butt. He spent hour after hour, session after session, just watching Jack's thumb as it hit the gun. Then he would take his file and work off a bit here and there until the young man's thumb and the cocking piece fit together perfectly upon contact.

When Jack got the holster all tied down on his leg, it nested there like a part of him, leaving nothing in the way to impede the sweep of his hand as he slapped it down. It was a continual puzzlement to him that he would still be thinking "draw" when the Colt was pointed straight out at full cock.

"You got the feel for it, Little Jack. Born to it. I hope to high heaven you got a cool head to match it."

John kept him at it, drawing from all manner of positions—standing in a crouch, falling, laying down, running, rolling, sitting—even riding, at a walk and at a full run. It was pull, point, click. Pull, point, click. Jack's hands got so sore and stiff he was hard pressed to hold a coffee cup, but John did not let him slack off on the practice. And every night he cleaned and oiled the gun, and soaped the holster. One evening when Jack balked at the boring, seemingly unnecessary routine, John told him, "Saw a gun blow up in a man's face once. He'd left it dirty. Gets around pretty good, for a blind man." Jack never complained again.

Only after Jack had mastered the draw and had learned to aim properly, did John dig into his pocket for the .44 cartridges.

It was more fun, shooting at targets, and they made a game of it. Jack could draw as quickly as John, but he could not match his skill at hitting the empty tins, bottles, and limbs they shot at. The standing targets became easy for him, for he had a natural eye, but the moving shots left him disgusted with himself. John could pluck a thrown rock from the air four out of five times. Jack was fortunate to hit one in five. His hand toughened to the draw, but now his wrists became sore from the recoil. They kept at it.

One morning as Jack rolled from his bedroll to the smell of coffee perking, he saw that John had loaded up the packhorse.

"I've taught you what I can. You're ready. You are good, Little Jack, better than most. And you'll get better yet. But the rest will be up to you. Just keep at it.

"It's time we were after them lowlife McCabes."

Chapter Eight

They met the pilgrims at the Red River. Two men in suits and brand new Texas hats that had never held a horse's fill of water.

They sat on the spring seat of a closed wagon, mired to the hubs in the sands of the river. One of them, the smaller of the two, was leaned over the side, staring at the sluggish red waters, as if by watching he might will the wheels of the wagon to turn. The other man—a ponderous, hulking behemoth with a porcine face, heavy shoulders and a ballooning belly—was lashing at the struggling team of horses with a long-handled whip, screaming a string of cusswords that would set a river pirate to blushing. John and Jack halted their animals on the high bank and sat watching. John's jaw tensed at the treatment the lathered team was receiving.

The smaller man spotted the riders and nudged his partner with an elbow. The driver looked up then, smiled, and tipped his hat.

"You kill those horses, mister," John said calmly, "you'll never get that rig out of there."

73

"Good day, my friends. Might we prevail upon your good natures for assistance?" the big man asked.

"Don't know as I've got one," John said, then added, "Reckon we could give you a hand, but you're going to have to get your feet wet."

Hesitantly, the pair climbed off the wagon seat and waded to the bank.

"Phineas Blackwater," the big man said, a gold tooth gleaming in his forced smile. He extended a pudgy hand. "And this is my associate, Floyd Fish. We are merchants, just come from Missouri."

Jack smiled at the odd combination of names. Fish and Blackwater. John ignored Blackwater's proffered hand.

"Your wagon loaded?"

The drummers exchanged concerned glances, then acknowledged that it was. John swung down from his mount. Jack's boots hit the turf a heartbeat later.

"We'll make a line from the back of the wagon to the bank. We can pass your cargo along."

John Dancer removed his boots and set them to the side. Then he took his gunbelt from around his waist and hung it over the saddle horn on the black. He waded into the water.

"Little Jack, you stay on the bank. We'll pass the goods forward. You stack it out of the way of the team."

Blackwater plunged back into the water, hurrying past John to the back of the wagon, saying, "I'm taller. I'll take the gate."

The cargo was twenty-four cases of cheap whiskey. The men passed the crates in relay to the shore.

"That's the lot," Blackwater said finally. John turned and waded toward the river bank.

Blackwater reached again to the back of the wagon and drew out a rifle, bringing the muzzle to bear on the back of John Dancer.

"Tell the boy to drop his weapon."

Fish reached quickly inside his coat and pulled out a two-shot derringer, covering Jack.

"I'm afraid we cannot allow you gentlemen to precede us to civilization, knowing our cargo, though we appreciate your kind assistance. We will require your strong backs to finish our chore—Boy, I said drop your weapon!"

Jack reached to the buckle at his waist. Fish cocked the little sleeve gun.

Jack's six-gun was in his hand and bucking. Blackwater's rifle went flying into the river as the .44 slug tore through his shoulder. Startled, Fish whipped his head around toward his partner and Jack delivered him a matching wound. The little gun fell on the bank.

John left the water's edge, detouring to step on Fish's firearm and to sink it into the red mud and out of sight. He sat down on the grass and pulled on his boots, then strapped on his gun. He walked over to Jack, who still stood with his gun drawn, covering the whiskey peddlers. John slapped him on the shoulder.

"You did fine, partner. Put it away now."

John crossed to the pile of crates in the grassy flat above the shoreline and began to open the boxes. When he had the crates open, John pulled his pistol, reversed it and began smashing the bottles with the butt. Blackwater, looking distressed, started for dry ground.

"No, stop, you son of a—"

John's hard glare cut off Blackwater's protest.

"Stay where you're at, fat man."

When he had finished destroying the whiskey runners' inventory, John mounted and signaled for Jack to do the same. Then he motioned for Blackwater to come out of the river. Fish was huddled on the bank, pressing a handkerchief to his wound and whining pitifully.

"You surely aren't going to leave us here like this?" Blackwater fell to his knees on the muddy bank.

John drew his Colt and brandished it toward the big man's head.

"It's hot weather for grave digging, but it's your call."

Blackwater and Fish stared in alarm, then dove for the water. They splashed and floundered, fleeing for the protection of the wagon.

The Dancer men rode off laughing.

The crackling flames of the campfire sent forth a dancing circle of light to do battle with the oncoming shadows of night as the last red line of sunset settled behind the slumbering silhouette of the dark, rambling plain.

Jack climbed from a creek bed carrying a coffee pot and settled it into the embers at the edge of the fire. He dumped a heaping handful of coffee beans into the toe of an old sock that he carried for the purpose, laid the sock on a flat rock and, using another rock, began to pound, pulverizing the beans. He dumped the contents into the mouth of the pot, gingerly flipped shut the hinged lid with an index finger, and settled back on his haunches to watch the vapor rising from the spout.

The frogs in the creek bottom cleared their throats and began to sing as sweetly as nightbirds. Jack slapped at a mosquito, leaving a bloody smear on his neck, then scooted closer to the fire in the hope that the smoke would discourage the insect's loved ones from visiting the scene of the execution.

John sat across the fire from his nephew, puffing easily on an old clay pipe and watching the blue smoke from the bowl rush to join that from the flames in its climb for the heavens. Most men who rode the range nowadays preferred to roll their own, but John was partial to his pipe. Jack had never developed a taste for tobacco, but he enjoyed sharing the comfortable aroma of his uncle's habit.

"John, what'll we do once we get to Mobeetie?"

"Reckon we'll play 'er as she comes. First off, we'll look up Temple Houston, see if he's been able to find out anything."

"The marshal said he's a district attorney? What's that?"

"Well, it's a lawyer appointed to prosecute criminals in a designated area."

"Is this Mister Houston a good friend of yours?"

"Temp? I'd like to think so, though we've sort of lost touch with one another the last few years. You've heard of *Sam* Houston," John said.

"Sure, the Raven. Led the army of Texas in the war against Mexico."

John nodded. "Well, Temp's his youngest, of four sons and four daughters. Temple Houston was the first baby ever born in the Governor's Mansion in Austin."

"How'd you come to know him?" Jack asked. "I don't figger you'd run into him at no Governor's Ball."

John smiled and hurled a stick at Jack from across the fire.

"Met him when he was just a colt. Old Sam had died when Temple was three years old, and his ma passed on four years later, so Temp went to live with his sister, Nannie, and her husband.

"He run off from there when he was twelve, already man-sized and raw-boned. Hopped his pony and took off to the cattle ranges on the Colorado and Concho rivers, west of Waco. That was in seventy-two.

"I was busting broncs over that way then, ranch-hopping from one spread to the other. All the ranchers around hooked up the next spring and put together a herd for a drive up to Bismark in the Dakota Territory, and I signed on. That's where I met up with Temple Houston."

John paused and knocked the dottle from his pipe into the palm of his hand and tossed it into the fire.

"Like I said, he was just a boy, but doing a man's work, and we made that drive together. I was known to be a fair hand with a gun, and young Temp wanted to learn how to shoot, so I taught him. He took right to it, like you did, and he's good. Real good.

"The men all liked him, for he was a talker, always spinning yarns around the fire of an evenin'. And he'd draw pictures for us. Loved to sketch. Always carried paper in his possibles. Here, I'll show you . . ."

John reached behind him and pulled his saddlebags to his side. He dug out an oilskin pouch, withdrew a yellowed scrap of paper, unfolded it, and handed it across to Jack. It was a charcoal drawing of his Uncle John in a shooter's stance, an excellent likeness, skillfully rendered. Jack likened it to those pictures he had seen in books at school.

"When we reached Dakota, I stayed on up there, wintered in Fargo. Worst decision I ever made, outside of me and Tom signing on with General McIntosh's cavalry. Spent the whole darn winter either up to my tail in snow or snuggled up next to a pot-bellied stove, dryin' my socks and thawin' toes."

"What about Houston?" Jack asked. "He stay with you?"

"Nope, the boy had more sense. After the drive, he got hired on as a clerk on a steamboat and sailed down to New Orleans."

"Must've been pretty smart to get a job like that, no older than he was."

"Smart? I hope to shout. He met up with an old political crony of his daddy's in New Orleans, and the man got him an appointment as a page in the Senate. He worked there in Washington City 'til he was sixteen, then came back here to Texas to go to college. Went to Texas A&M a while, then switched over to Baylor. That boy went through higher learnin' like a dose of salts. He stampeded through a four year course in nine months. Graduated with honors.

"I ran into him again three years ago in Brazoria, down on the Gulf. Had him a nice law practice goin' for himself and engaged to marry up with some pretty little rich girl, name of Laura somethin' or 'other. And him still only nineteen years old.

"Yes, Little Jack, he's more than smart. Brilliant, I'd say. Knows Homer and Tacitus by heart, quotes from Shakespeare and the Bible . . . and that poet, Byron. Speaks Spanish and French like he was born to it, and at last count he could talk your leg off in seven different Indian tongues."

Jack did not know what Homer or Tassy-whatever were, but he did not ask. He did not want to interrupt John's telling about Houston, he was that fascinated.

"They say folks will travel a hundred miles or more just to see him try a case, he puts on such a show."

Just then, a piece of firewood exploded with a crack like a rifle shot, sending a live coal streaking like a meteor into the darkness. Both men slapped at their guns. They looked at one another across the fire and burst out laughing.

"Will we get to see Houston perform in court?" Jack asked, still grinning.

John shrugged. "Don't know. But you'll meet him. Now pour me a cup of that good coffee 'fore it all boils away."

It occurred to Jack that the name on the sign post at the side of the road leading to town could be substituted with "Dodge City" or "Fort Worth," and nobody would be the wiser.

Mobeetie, a Comanche word meaning "sweet water", was a collection of unremarkable residences scattered haphazardly on the low hillsides surrounding a three-block long main street of false-fronted businesses. Atop a knoll overlooking the town stood a two-story rock courthouse and jail, appearing very austere against the steel-gray canvas of a cloudless sky. If there was a tree within a hard day's ride, Jack could not venture a guess on where it might be.

On a hill a mile out they could see the ordered ranks of structures that constituted Fort Elliot, dancing restlessly behind a shimmering curtain of heat. It was a rectangular fort with stables and parade ground attached. John told Jack that the stark military post was manned by black infantry and white cavalry, referred to by the locals as "salt 'n pepper soldier boys."

The angry sun that hurled its issue down upon the sweaty backs and blistered necks of the weary riders had not succeeded in slowing the commerce of Mobeetie. Although the mercury hovered several notches above the century mark, the dirt street was bustling with activity. Carriages, wagons, drays, mules, and horses moved along, unmindful of the scurrying forms of pedestrians darting from walk to walk, frantic as hornets in a jar. A brisk wind with the searing breath of a blast furnace whisked the dust dislodged by hooves, wheels, and boots into a soupy brown haze that hung hat-high the length of the town's lone thoroughfare.

They rode in at a walk, stopping at Clampitt's Livery to stable the animals, then shouldered their saddlebags, palmed their rifles, and walked next door to the Huselby House.

A buxom woman clerk sat red-faced on a high stool behind the registration desk. Her left hand was busy with a pasteboard fan, decorated with a fading lithograph of *The Last Supper,* aimed at her flushed cheeks. She had an index finger sunk to the second joint in the high lace collar of her blouse and traveling in a half-orbit from one side of her neck to the other. John Dancer walked to the desk and dropped his gear to the hardwood floor.

"Two rooms?" Her query lacked enthusiasm.

"One'll do."

The woman slid off the stool like molasses off a spoon, plopped open a black book, dipped the nib of a pen into an ink well, and handed it to John.

"Dollar for the room. Fifty cents if you want a bath. Extra quarter for fresh water."

John laid a dollar six-bits on the countertop as she bent beneath the counter and came out with a pair of folded towels. She turned and took a key off a board on the wall behind her.

"Number four, second door on your right down that hall. Bathroom's down at the end." The clerk looked at the signature in the book as John bent to pick up his gear.

"John Dancer . . . ? Any gun trouble you got in mind, appreciate your taking it outside."

"No trouble," he said, taking the comment in stride. "Know where I might find Temple Houston?"

"Lives at the Grand Central Hotel in the next block, but you'll more likely find him down at the Cattle Exchange Saloon. Ever' Friday, him and Judge Willis and a group of other lawyers and peace officers get up a poker game. Be there all night, most likely."

Chapter Nine

The sun had gone below the undulate horizon, but the oppressive heat still hung heavy between the false-fronted buildings lining both sides of the main street of Mobeetie. The Dancers were sweating again by the time they pushed aside the batwings and entered the Cattle Exchange Saloon. They had bathed, then rested awhile before wolfing down fried steak and potatoes in the dining room of the Huselby House. Both men felt revitalized now, and Jack was eager to meet Houston.

A burly bouncer with his arms folded across a massive chest directed them to an area of private rooms at the rear of the saloon, so they worked their way across the crowded floor and came to a halt outside a curtained alcove. Brocaded drapes were pulled back against the side walls of the little room.

Seven men sat at a round table covered with green felt, playing poker. A sizable, multi-colored mound of chips was heaped in the center of the table. John indicated the broad back of one of the players with his thumb and whispered in Jack's ear.

Just then a ruckus broke out at the bar. A squat, little drunk in a derby hat was complaining loudly.

"You son of a sore-ridden, louse-infested, pock-marked trollop . . . you've been waterin' me drinks all evenin'. I want me money's worth!"

One of the poker players in the alcove, a large man with a drooping walrus mustache and a Sheriff's badge pinned to his vest, looked to another man lounging against the opposite wall watching the game. He motioned him toward the disturbance with a long black cigar in the crook of his forefinger. The lean deputy pushed himself away from the wall with a booted foot and ambled over to the bar. He drew his pistol, reversed it in his fist, then picked the hard-shelled derby from the drunk's head. The lawman brought the butt of his gun crashing down on a bare circle on top of the troublemaker's skull. The little inebriate bounced off the bar and back into the deputy, who grabbed him under the arms and dragged him to a chair against the wall at the end of the bar. He propped up the unconscious offender so that he would not slide to the floor, then walked back to resume his stance against the alcove wall. Of the players at the table, only the sheriff's attention had been drawn from the cards by the commotion.

John Dancer, meanwhile, had been watching the dealer, a man with a glass eye, who had been skillfully manipulating the cards by slipping himself the second card in the deck. John thought the others in the game unaware of the dealer's sleight of hand, but the big man with his back to them, the man he had pointed out to Jack, suddenly brought his six-gun from beneath the table and laid it on the green felt playing surface.

"If I catch any sonofagun cheating," the man said calmly, "I'll shoot out his other eye."

The one-eyed dealer chuckled and threw the errant card face up on the table.

"Just seeing if you were on your toes, Houston."

All the players laughed then, as the game apparently was not a terribly serious one. John Dancer stepped forward.

"Howdy, Temp."

The big man spun around, the gun appearing in his hand as if by magic.

"John! By the gods, it's good to see you."

Temple Houston sprang to his feet and smothered the smaller man in a gigantic hug. John extricated himself, and, blushing, stepped back a step to pump his friend's hand.

Jack had expected Houston to be someone larger than life, and he was not disappointed. He saw a man standing six foot two, slightly stooped, clean shaven, with a swarthy look about him. His auburn hair fell in curling locks to his wide shoulders. He was wearing a finely tailored, extra-long frock coat over a yellow, beaded vest, Spanish style satin-striped trousers with a bell flare and small box-toed riding boots of the finest leather. He had a large face and small, intense eyes of gray. Strapped to his lean hips in a fancily embossed holster rode the magical nickel-plated Colt revolver with carved ivory grips.

"Temp," John said, "I want you to meet Little Jack, my nephew and partner."

They shook hands and exchanged salutations, then Houston turned back to the table and introduced them to his poker-playing friends. At the mention of John Dancer's name, the lawmen gathered at the table perked up, exchanging knowing glances with the other players.

The men in the alcove would have been an impressive group by virtue of sheer physical size alone. District Judge Frank Willis loomed largest of them all; he was well over six feet and nearly three hundred pounds. Jim Browning and Colonel Grigsby, an ex-Quantrill man, were both lawyers, both about the same height and build as Houston. The Sheriff, Henry Fleming, was a tall Irishman who was also a saloonkeeper and a gambler. County Judge F. M. Patton, who had been a soldier and buffalo hunter, was also a large man. The only one of the group smaller than Jack was the lawyer Woodman, whose glass eye gave him a perpetual expression of surprise. An aura of power seemed to emanate from the cramped room.

"Deal me out, gentlemen. My friend and I have some catching up to do."

After excusing himself from the game, Houston ushered the Dancers to one of the adjoining alcoves, then motioned across the room to the bartender. A pretty, little, Mexican serving girl in a full, gaily colored skirt and a simple, white, off-the-shoulder blouse came to take their orders.

John and Houston launched immediately into reminiscences of shared adventures. Jack leaned forward, elbows on the table, listening eagerly to the rambling intercourse, so liberally spiced with laughter. The girl returned with a bucket of cold beer and three empty mugs. While the other two talked on, Jack poured and distributed the beers. Into the third bucket, they had pretty much covered the trail drive all the way to Dakota. John turned to his nephew with a mischievous twinkle in his brown eyes.

"Jack, see that fancy white-handled pistol on Temple's hip? He named that gun 'Ol' Betsy.' Seems to me a man that names his gun has got a lot of time on his hands . . . or he's a mighty lonely man."

Houston leaned back in his chair, folded his hands across his vest and smiled.

"Well now, John. Seems I remember a little ol' gal in Caldwell, Kansas had a few pet names for you. 'Ol' Big Boy,' she called you, and 'Honey Lips.' I could never get a woman to call me such sweet names, so I was reduced to christening my sidearm."

John Dancer's face took on a scarlet hue, and all three men laughed heartily.

"That little gal was a caution, wasn't she? I bring her to mind almost every time I shake out my blankets."

Jack shared some of the things that had occurred on his drive from Buffalo Springs to Dodge City, and the three of them talked their way into the evening. Finally, Jack broached the subject of the McCabe brothers.

"They have not been to Mobeetie, Jack, of that I'm certain. I know most everyone in town, and I made a thorough survey after receiving John's letter." Houston turned his attention to John.

"Judge Willis and I must travel to Tascosa in two days time to try a docket of cases, and that town's reputation and personality would be a stronger magnet for men on the dodge than even Mobeetie. Come with us. I will aid you in your search.

"In the meantime, men, I suggest you ride to Palo Duro Canyon and seek Charles Goodnight's counsel. It may be that some of his hands have heard or seen something."

Houston took a paper from his inside coat pocket and extended it to John Dancer. "This will introduce you to Mister Goodnight. He can point you at who best to talk with.

"Then come back here and we'll check out Tascosa."

John and Jack Dancer lingered at the table in the saloon. Houston had excused himself, explaining that he had a brief to prepare for the next day's session of court. And John had plans for his nephew—a trip to Feather Hill, the name given to the thriving section of fancy houses on the northwest side of town, an area that most of Mobeetie's respectable citizens avoided.

There were at least thirteen brothels in the Feather Hill section, all prospering under the guidance of madams with colorful names like Belle of Mo-beetie, Little Queen, Red Nellie, Frog-Mouth Annie, and Ella Brown, The Diamond

Girl. This "bald-headed whiskey town" was a gathering place for cowboys and drovers, bullwhackers and mule-skinners, wolfers and hiders from a hundred miles of prairie in every direction, and all had the same lean stamp. They came with pockets jingling and appetites to be whetted, and Feather Hill cheerfully accommodated each and every one.

The Dancers made the rounds, stopping in several establishments, observing the drinking, gambling, and other activities taking place in plush parlors, saloons, and dance halls, all with gaudy hostesses on display, all with dozens of ways to separate their fun-seeking clientele from their hard-earned money.

It was not a practice frowned on, in this day and time, for a single man to take his pleasures when and where he found them, for life on the frontier was hard, and often of short duration. Yet John wanted to impress upon young Jack the pitfalls that awaited the unwary and uninitiated beneath the glitter in such places.

"It's easy for a lonely man to get tempted into what looks like innocent fun," John warned, "but you can lose your bankroll or your life faster than a snake's strike on streets like these . . . And every frontier town's got 'em."

Jack smiled and turned to face his uncle.

"No need to worry on my account," he said. "Tom taught me about such things years ago. I don't have to do something foolhardy to prove to myself or to the world that I'm a man. I reckon I've still got some growin' up to do, but I'll let it happen natural. I don't have to go lookin' for it."

John slapped him on the back and said, "Boy, I reckon I won't be callin' you *Little* Jack ever again."

For hours they had seen nothing in front of their horse's noses but the parched tabletop expanse of the high plain: stove-lid flat and boundless, empty of all but gray soil and dry grass. Suddenly they saw a dark slash across the land

and the Dancers found themselves on the brink of a spectacular gorge. The prairie was carved away to a depth of seven-hundred feet, forming a fifteen-thousand-acre canyon of plunging walls, incredible spires, and pinnacles standing brilliant in the sun. Multicolored layers of soil and rock joined the greens and grays of cedar, mesquite, sage, and wild china to form a palette so breathtakingly colorful and scenic that it sent a tingle of excitement through Jack's entire body.

This was the Palo Duro Canyon, absolute domain of cattle baron Charles Goodnight.

In 1874, Colonel Mackenzie had led the troops of the Fourth Cavalry in a sweep across the high plains in pursuit of Comanches who had broken from their reservation in Indian Territory, and who were then menacing a wide area. He defeated the proud plains warriors here, in their camp in the Palo Duro, in the last great Indian battle in Texas.

Goodnight had grown up on the Brazos—neighbor to the likes of George Slaughter and Shanghai Pierce—an ordinary cowpoke that knew how to follow swallows to find a water hole. He knew to suck a bullet when he was thirsty, or to stave off hunger by chewing tobacco. He'd been a man who ate prairie dog stew so as not to starve.

When the war came, Goodnight joined the Texas Rangers, serving as a scout and guide, fending off Comanches and Kiowas on the western frontier. He mustered out in '64, built a herd using credit and a discreet running iron, then teamed up with a man named Loving, who was killed a year later by Comanches, over on the Pecos. Goodnight and Loving blazed a cattle trail to the mining camps and military posts in Colorado. With profits from the drive, Goodnight bought property along the Arkansas, near Pueblo, and stocked it with another drive up from Texas.

By 1873, Charles Goodnight was one of the richest cattlemen in Colorado. To fight high interest rates, he formed his own bank, but his empire crumbled in the great crash of '73, and he was faced with beginning again.

Penniless, he turned his eyes again to Texas, and in 1874, already famous as a pioneer cattle driver and stockman, Charlie Goodnight drove sixteen hundred head of cattle, remnants of his Colorado herd, to the Palo Duro Canyon. Now he ruled not only the canyon, but the outlying plains, farther than a man could see. The JA herd now numbered well over one hundred thousand animals, and his second fortune was made. Goodnight had dispensed a hard justice in his domain before the law came to the Llano Estacada, battling homesteaders and small ranchers with hanging hemp and a gun.

"There's the ranch headquarters over there."

John pointed out across the canyon to a distant village of fifty or so structures peeking out of the haze to the east, and they headed that way, walking their horses along the steep bluff of the chasm. After a few miles, they found a trail leading down and bottomed out on a vast, sheltered, well-watered pasture, fenced naturally by the steep canyon walls.

As they neared the village, the riders could hear the myriad sounds of a working ranch—the ring of a smithy's hammer, men shouting, cow bells clanging, trace chains rattling, horses snorting and neighing, dogs barking, and the lowing of cattle.

When the Dancers reached the village, a *vaquero,* lounging in the shade of the blacksmith shop waiting for his horse to be shod, aimed them toward a two-story house on the other end of the courtyard. They made their way past a mess house and a dairy to the big plank and log headquarters, where they were greeted at the door by another Mexican. This was Goodnight's home, and he kept his office here. John handed the letter of introduction from Houston to the house boy and he hurried off into the interior.

He returned shortly to escort the Dancer men into a spacious office.

"Be right with you."

Charlie Goodnight was a bowlegged, bearded, bull of a man. He had his back to them, hanging a magnificent set of mounted horns on the wall behind a massive, rustic desk. He spoke to them over his shoulder.

"Old Blue just died. These were his horns. Best damn lead steer to ever move a herd up a trail."

The rancher stepped backward off a short stool, took another step back to admire his work, brushed his palms together, and turned to face his visitors.

"Now, men, how can I help you?" Goodnight eased into a high-backed overstuffed, leather swivel chair behind the desk. He clasped his hands on the desktop before him. "John Dancer, is it?"

"Yes, sir. I'm John, this is my nephew and partner, Jack Dancer.

"We're looking for four men, Mister Goodnight. Fugitives, brothers by the name of McCabe."

"You are lawmen, then?"

"No, sir. This is personal."

"Well, I got no doubt you're in the right, whatever the trouble. Lawyer Houston speaks mighty highly of you. But boys, I don't know how much good I can do you. The JA is a mighty big spread. I've lost count of all the acres I run cows on, and we have outposts scattered over the entire range. If these men you're looking for were only drifting through and didn't stop right here, I might never hear of it. Mind tellin' me what these ol' boys did to get you so riled?"

John leaned his head toward Jack. "Jack here can tell it better'n I can. It started with him."

Jack told Goodnight the entire story, forward from the

night of the gunfight in Buffalo Springs, finishing with what the McCabes had done to his mother and to Tom.

"Yankee scum! Tell you what boys, if you can catch up to 'em, bring 'em back by here and I'll hang 'em all for you. What do they look like?"

"One of them is an albino, sir. No color to him. The others—"

"Wait a minute," Goodnight said. "Vasquez seen them then, over in Tascosa. About a week ago, it was. He came back after a trip over there, carryin' on about seein' this funny lookin' hombre with pink skin and white hair, like one of them little bunny rabbits they got up north where it's cold."

"Could we talk to this Vasquez, sir?"

"Sure can. He ought to be in here about sundown. In the meantime, let's get you boys somethin' to eat under your belts. Supper ought to be about ready."

"Much obliged, sir," John said, "if it wouldn't put you out none."

Goodnight waved the thought off.

"You happened by on the right day, boys. We're having a pork roast tonight." The rancher rubbed his flat belly in anticipation.

"Pork?" Jack blurted out.

Goodnight chuckled. "You bet. Them beeves are to sell, not to eat."

After they had eaten, they talked to the Mexican, Vasquez. He could add little to the fact that he had indeed seen the men they sought in Tascosa one week ago, and that all four of the brothers were still traveling together. Jack and John walked back to the house to thank the Goodnights for their hospitality.

"Mary Ann said she'd have my hide if I let you boys ride out of here tonight," the rancher told them. "Let us put you up 'til morning. You can get a fresh start with some of Miz Goodnight's good cookin' behind you."

"We wouldn't want to put you out," John told him. "Besides, we're planning on goin' to Tascosa with Temple Houston in the morning."

"No trouble at all. Mary Ann enjoys fussin' over folks. And here at the ranch you're closer to Tascosa than you are to Mobeetie. You can meet your friend there."

When the cock crowed the next morning, Mary Ann Goodnight had steak and eggs, biscuits and gravy on the table, and she had packed a lunch for the Dancers to take along with them to eat on the trail.

As they topped out on the plain, Jack reined around to look back over the canyon. It was the darnedest sight he had ever seen. And those were good people down there. He thought about his ma and Tom, and a great sense of shame rushed over him. Here he was admiring the scenery while the McCabes were still running free.

Jack Dancer drew his Colt .44 and checked the loads in the cylinder.

"Let's go to Tascosa."

Chapter Ten

Blackjack Daniels, alias Phineas Blackwater, stepped off the stage in Tascosa, wincing at the jarring pain in his shoulder as his booted foot hit the ground. He reached up with his left arm to receive his duffel from the driver on top of the coach.

"Cross-eyed sonofagun must have hit every bump between here and Fort Worth," he muttered to himself.

The hired killer relinquished the bag to the eager fingers of the Mexican boy who came rushing forth, then headed for a sign down the street that offered *ROOMS—50¢*. The niño fell in behind, struggling with the heavy luggage and skipping to keep up with the señor's long strides.

Blackjack checked in and climbed the narrow stairs to his second floor room. He took the bag from the boy, flipped him a coin, then slammed the door shut on the grinning brown face. He tossed his hat onto the cracked and peeling top of an ancient bureau and pulled a long, green cigar from his pocket. He bit off the tip, spit it away, and brought the cigar to life on the flame of a sulfur match.

The springs of the bed complained loudly as Blackjack lowered himself to a sitting position on the edge of the mattress. He slid his right arm gingerly out of the sling around his neck and flexed his pudgy, sausage-like fingers to restore the circulation. Leaving the arm free, he eased himself down onto the pillow and lay back, staring at the irregularly shaped yellow stains the leaky roof had bequeathed the ceiling. *Jehosaphat,* it was hot.

Blackjack figured if he had done this deal his way to begin with, John Dancer and the kid would be dead by now and he would be in a cool, quiet saloon somewhere nursing a beer—instead of laying here in this blistering annex of Hades nursing a hole in his blasted shoulder. McCabe and his confounded, complicated strategies for preserving appearances! It had been a fool notion, posing as a whiskey peddler in trouble. Still, it had almost worked. But who knew that snot-nosed kid could shoot like that? Blackjack had not even seen his hand go for the gun. And that fool Fish, the man Dad McCabe had hired to side him, had been worthless as a meek mute at a hog-calling contest. It had been a pleasure to leave the little weasel stranded on the Red, wounded and crying.

Old man McCabe wanted the entire Dancer family dead, so things would simmer down and he could bring his sons home. The old lady and her one-armed, invalid son had been easy. Blackjack had smothered them both with the same pillow. Hadn't left a mark on either of them. The man had surprised him some, fighting until the last moment like he did. But it was done, and when the bodies were discovered, folks figured the son had died and the old lady had keeled over with her heart from the grief.

McCabe was paying him very well, a small fortune to a man used to skinning by. That's why he had agreed to the old man's schemes. From now on though, Blackjack Daniels would do it his way, safe from ambush, like he had always done.

He tried to count up in his head how many men he had

killed for pay. The Rebs that he had picked off as a sniper during the war did not count. Nor did he credit himself with the Indians he had left sprawled on the plains as a buffalo hunter—some because they were shooting at him, some just for fun. Hardly nobody counted Indians, anyhow.

When he finished this assignment, Blackjack figured to go back East somewhere, buy himself a brothel or a barroom, and live off the returns.

He would meet tonight with the old man's sons, shoo them out of town and out of the way. They were to wait in Denver for word from Dad McCabe—he would send them money to live on until it was safe for them to return to Texas.

After that, he would locate John Dancer and the boy and kill them both. He intended to catch them separated, do them one at a time. With his bad wing, Daniels did not relish facing either man head on.

In any case, Blackjack did not expect his intended victims would be able to recognize him. He had discarded those fancy dude's rags and was now wearing his own, more familiar, greasy buckskins. And he was allowing his beard to grow back in. He had always felt more comfortable with a full face of hair.

The leather-bound assassin hauled his heavy frame off the bed. He slipped his arm back into the sling, grabbed his slouch hat, and walked through the door, headed out to locate the McCabe brothers.

As he hit the boardwalk in front of the inn, Daniels saw two mounted men walking their horses, a black and a buckskin, down the center of the street, headed in the direction of the courthouse in the square. John and Jack Dancer.

He stood his ground as they passed within four feet of his position. Neither man gave him a second glance.

Blackjack Daniels allowed himself a rare smile.

The village of Tascosa lay sprawled along the north bank of the Canadian River, its sun-dried adobe structures blend-

ing with the drab, ochre-colored background of the surrounding prairie.

The wide wooden bridge that spanned the river was
crowded with a slow-moving stream of creaking donkey
carts, cowboys on horseback, burros with their backs piled
high with goods, and straight-backed women with ollas and
baskets balanced atop their heads. The river was low, so
rather than join the herd of humanity on the bridge, Jack
and John urged their horses over the sandy bank and into
the water, mindful to keep them moving to avoid the
treacherous quicksand that pocketed the channel.

As they entered the streets of Tascosa, the plaintive
rhythm of strummed guitars and the soft strains of love
songs sung in liquid Spanish caressed their ears. Bright red
garlands of peppers hung from the roughhewn timbers of
adobe huts and the tantalizing smell of baked tortillas per-
meated the air. Bands of brown, barefoot children dashed
through the dusty streets, whooping like happy bandidos,
with scruffy puppies bounding after them in joyous, yip-
ping pursuit.

Tascosa proudly called itself the "Cowboy Capitol of the
Plains." Others called it "The Bloodiest Place in Texas."
As with most rawhide frontier towns of the day, Tascosa
was divided by an imaginary, but perceptible, line that separated the "respectable" sector to the north from the livelier,
dirtier, lustier area along the river. This latter section was
called "Hogtown," because the residents acted like swine
and visitors came away hog-drunk.

The Dancer men made their way to the courthouse on
the square in the center of town. They learned that Houston
and his party had not yet arrived, so they left word with a
clerk that they were in town and would return later.

Following the delectable aroma of broiling meat, they
reined up in front of a small cantina. They stood down and
wrapped their reins around a rail at the door. Jack had to

stoop to avoid cracking his skull on the low portal as they entered the dim interior.

The mestizo host served them up ponderous portions of *cabrito*—barbecued goat, *caldo de pollo*—chicken broth, enchiladas, chili and frijoles, and tall glasses of chilled sangria. They leaned over the heaping platters and attacked the feast with unbridled gusto.

Meanwhile, across town, five men sat in huddled conversation around a table in a dark corner of a noisy saloon. Cash McCabe was gesturing wildly, obviously angry.

"If they're here in town, I ain't leavin'. Nobody is killing Jack Dancer but me!"

Blackjack Daniels' features darkened and he leaned his buckskin-clad bulk across the scarred table top, stopping in Cash's face.

"Your daddy wants you out of this. Your daddy wants you gone. What you boys did at the Dancer farm was stupid, and it's been left to me to pull your irons out of the fire. Get out of Texas, McCabe, and let me do my job."

Cash started out of his chair and reached for his gun. Oran's great hand darted out to clamp around his brother's wrist. He squeezed and Cash cried out, his features distorted with pain.

"The man told you, Cash, what Dad said to do. It ain't just your hide you'd be putting at risk. All four of us is in this together. We'll go on up to Colorado like Dad wants. You can ride sitting up, or tied across your saddle, but you are goin'."

As Oran released his grip, Cash jerked back his arm and plopped down in his chair, rubbing his wrist and glowering at his brother through narrowed lids, like a chastened child.

"We're 'bout out of money," Gunter said in a nasal whine. "What're we supposed to do, live off the land?"

Blackjack stood up and dug into a buckskin pouch at his

waist. He pulled out a sheaf of bills and peeled off a stack. He tossed the money onto the table.

"There's a hundred apiece for traveling money. Write me out a receipt. I'll get it back from your old man."

The hired gunman produced a pencil stub and a scrap of paper. Oran scribbled out the necessary notation and handed it to Blackjack, then he pocketed the pile of bills.

"Leave tonight, soon as it gets dark," Blackjack told them. "You'll be got in touch with when it's safe for you to be in Texas."

He lumbered for the door.

Jack and John were sitting on the courthouse steps, waiting, when Houston's buggy pulled up in front. Houston waved, then waited while Judge Willis hoisted his elephantine body off the padded bench and lowered himself in stages to the ground. Then the lawyer hopped off the opposite side of the buggy and handed the reins to a young black man who had rushed out to meet them.

They shook hands all around and started to climb the steps to the courthouse door when Houston was hailed from behind.

"Temple Houston! Prepare to face a better man."

Three men spun as one. John Dancer, Temple Houston, and Jack Dancer stood crouched on the steps with guns cocked and level. They faced Bat Masterson, his hands held high, the tips of his lavish mustache tilted skyward by a broad grin.

A smile took command of Houston's face and he holstered his gun. Jack and John followed suit.

"Bat! What lured you down here to Tascosa? Must be money in it for you somewhere."

Masterson lowered his arms, tugged at the coattails of his black, tailor-made suit, and adjusted the high curled brim of his bowler hat.

"Now, Temp," Masterson replied, "is that any way to greet a friend that has ridden all the way from Denver to give you an opportunity to enhance your standing in the community?"

Houston gave him a suspicious glance. "Okay, what's up?"

"I got bored up there, Temple. I'm out of work, you know, since the good folks of Ford County voted me out of office up at Dodge last year. I figured we might set up a shooting match between you and me."

Before Houston could answer, two other men walked up to join them. The gent with the sheriff's badge pinned to his shirt was carrying a sawed-off shotgun in the crook of his right arm. The other man displayed a deputy's star and wore his gun low and tied down. Houston introduced the newcomers.

"Men, this is Sheriff Willingham . . . and his deputy, Henry Newton Brown," Houston said, indicating each in turn. Then he identified the Dancers for the lawmen. They already knew Masterson.

John was looking intently at the deputy.

"Brown. Of Lincoln County?"

"I been there," Brown said. "Heard of you, too."

Bat Masterson took charge then, turning the topic of conversation back to the proposed shooting match between Houston and himself. The lawyer agreed to the contest and they arranged to meet in one hour on the river bank below Hogtown.

"C'mon, Brown," Masterson said to the deputy, "you can help me get things set up."

Brown looked at the sheriff, who nodded his consent, then he and Bat Masterson walked off toward the river.

Houston and the Dancers arrived at the match site on schedule. Masterson had garnered a large crowd for the show. Any excuse for a bet was valid in a country where most men's days were filled only with tedium and toil. Any contest—a foot race, a boxfight, a shooting match, or the way the wind might blow—was reason aplenty.

Masterson and Deputy Brown had already warmed up the audience with a little contest of their own, and Bat was clutching a handful of greenbacks.

"You ready, Temple?" Bat asked him.

Houston nodded that he was. Brown had been drafted to throw the tin cans into the air. Each man was to be allowed five shots at his target. The shooter with the most hits would be the winner of that round. They flipped a coin to see who would shoot first.

Brown threw a tin can high in the air. Houston waited until the can was paused at the apex of its path, then drew his Colt, firing rapidly, the five reports so closely spaced that they sounded like a continual roll of thunder. A boy fetched the perforated target back to Brown. Five hits.

Masterson duplicated Houston's feat on his first try, and the two marksmen continued in the same manner, firing and reloading and firing again, for a full twenty minutes with neither man missing a shot.

Sensing a growing disinterest among the gathering of spectators, Brown switched to a different target. A plug of tobacco with a small star printed on the wrapper. One shot per man this time, the object being to hit as close as possible to the star. Houston was up first.

Brown sent the tobacco plug spinning into empty space. Houston drew and fired. The flung target jumped acrobatically as the bullet struck it on the fly. The boy lurched off at a lope to fetch the plug. As he plucked it from the river sand where it had landed, he let out a low whistle. Scurrying back through the press of spectators, he passed it to Brown, who examined it, then passed it along to Masterson.

Bat shook his head as he held the plug up to the light. A clean bullet hole now decorated the star, dead center.

"Can't improve on perfection," Masterson said, and he slid his gun into the holster on his hip as a gesture of concession. "Where'd you learn to shoot like that, Temp?"

Temple Houston reached to grab John around the shoulder. "This man taught me. John Dancer."

"Well then," Bat said, "I can't best you. Maybe he can. How about it, Dancer? You shoot against Houston."

John was embarrassed and hesitant, but at the urgings of Temple and his nephew, he reluctantly agreed. Bat reached in a pocket and withdrew two nickels. He handed the coins to Deputy Brown, who placed them on end atop two posts. The opponents assumed their stances, sixty yards from the tiny targets.

"When I drop my cane," Masterson said, "draw and fire as it hits the ground. Accuracy will be the determining factor, except in case of a tie. Then the speed of the draw will determine the winner."

The renowned lawman raised the decorous walking stick into the air to the full length of his arm, holding it aloft as a hush fell over the crowd of anxious spectators.

Masterson dropped the cane.

Both men drew. Their hands were matched blurs of flashing speed. Two shots rang out as one, and both coins disappeared from their perches. The crowd pushed forward. Brown held them back as the boy located Houston's coin. He held it aloft, grinning, then returned his eyes to search the sandy soil. He found the other coin and ran, holding the nickels in separate clenched fists, to Brown.

Brown examined the punctured targets for a long, agonizing moment, then held them aloft for all to see.

"A matched pair," he shouted, "Both coins right through the middle."

Chapter Eleven

Temple Houston was acquainted with every saloon and brothel in Hogtown—not as a customer, but as a prosecutor. The rugged and reckless men who frequented the various bars and bordellos of Tascosa had an habitual bent toward maiming and killing one another while under the combined influence of too much raw whiskey and the heady perfume of ready romance. As a result, nearly all of the barkeeps and madams and most of the working girls in the wide open frontier village had, at one time or other, been called to court as witnesses to murder or mayhem.

The Dancers had learned from the *vaquero*, Vasquez, that the McCabes had been in Tascosa little more than a week past. If the brothers were still in town, by all that's holy, they vowed to find them.

To the palaces of pleasure, the saloons, and the gambling halls of Hogtown they went, questioning dozens of satin-gowned strumpets in their velvet parlors, and legions of burly brutes who poured the whiskey in smoke-filled bar-rooms. They sought the help of dusty range riders fresh off the plains, and of the border wolves, smugglers, and bandits that frequented the dimly-lit dens of decadence along the river. No one would admit to having seen the McCabe brothers.

Despairing of ever finding them, the tired and thirsty trio stopped at a quiet neighborhood cantina. John and Temple seated themselves at a round table near the door. Jack walked to the bar and placed their order, then joined them. A rotund Anglo man with a bald head, yellow eyes, and rotting teeth, wearing the filthiest apron Jack had ever seen, rounded the end of the bar balancing a tray bearing three mugs of beer. More from the night's habit than of any hope of a positive response, Jack asked the oft-repeated question.

"You seen four men, one of them an albino?"

The barman shook his head, plucked fifteen cents from John's palm and shuffled back toward the bar.

"I seen 'em."

The voice came from a dark corner near the rear of the cantina. Three heads turned to face the anonymous volunteer. A tall, lanky cowboy emerged from the shadows and crossed toward them, weaving as he came.

Jack clambered to his feet and offered the tipsy Texan his seat at the table, then pulled up another chair, straddling it.

"Only there was five men, not four," the cowboy said.

"When? Where?" John asked.

"I could use a drink."

Jack motioned to the bald barkeep. "Bring this man a bottle of whiskey."

The slender cowhand sat quietly, a glazed look to his eyes, until the bottle and an empty glass were placed before him. Ignoring the glass, he pulled the cork with his teeth, spat it away, and took a long pull from the bottle of rye.

"Ahhh." He wiped his mouth with the back of his hand.

"They was right here, this afternoon. The barkeep seen 'em too."

John whipped his head around to see the barman's glistening dome disappearing through a curtained door.

"You know where they are now?"

The cowboy shrugged. "Heard them say somethin' about Colorado. The big man in buckskins told the other four to skedaddle, come dark. He give 'em some money."

"You sure of this?" Houston asked.

"I'm drunk now. Wasn't then. Four men, one of 'em a little feller with white hair to his shoulders. Had on a pair of them dark spectacles . . ."

"That's Gunter, for sure," Jack said.

"Then this big ol' boy in the hide suit come in. He wasn't one of them I don't think, but he knew 'em sure enough. He left 'em after he give 'em the money. They sat here 'til purt'nigh nighttime, then they lit out. Give the barkeep somethin' to say he hadn't seen 'em, should anybody ask."

They thanked him and walked outside. Disillusionment lay heavy on Jack's heart. They had missed the McCabes, and he could see nothing but endless trails and long days in the saddle ahead of them.

Houston had arranged for a room for John and Jack at the hotel in which he stayed when in Tascosa, and Jack wanted to call it a night. John had seen a girl at Mustang Mae's fancy house that he wanted to get to know better, so he gave Jack the room key and told him he would see him later. Houston wandered off on some similar mission of his own. Jack struck out alone for the hotel.

It was the middle of the night, but the strains of music and laughter hung heavy in the air, joined rudely by an occasional shot or scream. Jack walked the dark, narrow street, enjoying the solitude and the freshness of the open air after spending so much of the evening amid the clamorous, odoriferous atmosphere of Hogtown and its obsessive fun-seekers.

The sinister, metallic click of the cocking of a gun jerked

Jack's head toward a narrow, black recess between gray adobe walls. The glowing red eye of a cigar stared back at him. He dove heedlessly for cover as the flash from a muzzle caught the corner of his eye. Something tore his hat from his head, and a searing pain along his scalp arrived simultaneously with the booming report of a shot. He rolled as his shoulder hit the street and he came up firing, emptying his gun in a gut-high pattern that covered the dark passageway from wall to wall. He broke into a crouching run toward the adobe wall and slapped his shoulders flat against it. Jack peered cautiously into the alley. He reloaded his gun, then leapt across the opening to the next wall. He dug in his pocket for a match and raked it across the rough sand surface of the wall, squinting as it burst into flame. He could see nothing in the mouth of the alley. Gun at the ready, he moved forward, advancing slowly and cautiously down the narrow corridor. The alley was empty. Jack followed it to where it emptied onto another street, looked to both sides, and, seeing nothing, shrugged his shoulders. *Probably some drunk*, he thought as he retraced his steps. He headed again for the hotel.

Jack hung his Colt on the post of the headboard close to his pillow, peeled off his shirt, then sat on the edge of the bed to tug off his boots. He stepped out of his pants, letting them fall in a heap to the floor. Crossing to the mirror above the bureau, he inspected the new part in his hair. The bullet had scarcely burned him, but thinking of the near escape left him with a queasy feeling in the pit of his stomach.

Jack put a hand behind the chimney of the coal oil lamp on the night table and puffed out the flame. He lay back, and allowed his body to be swallowed in the folds of the feather mattress. By the time the doused wick of the lamp had quit smoking, Jack was asleep.

*   *   *

It had started to rain by the time Blackjack Daniels reached the hotel.

It had been bad luck, missing that shot from the alley, but the kid had reacted quickly and come up shooting. He was not about to stay around and shoot it out. Jack Dancer was too bloomin' fast on the trigger.

Daniels strolled in apparent innocence in front of the hotel, paused and peered through the glass-paneled door. As he had hoped, the desk clerk was leaned back in a chair, his feet propped on a shelf under the counter, his head laid back into a corner against the wall. The man was snoring loudly, and with each exhaled breath his mustache fluttered like a flag on a malodorous breeze. Carefully and quietly, Blackjack opened the door.

He crossed on tiptoe to the desk and ran a stubby finger down the roll of names in the register, then walked softly to the stairway and climbed to peer over the landing. The hallway was deserted, so he climbed on up and found room seven.

Blackjack tried the knob. Locked.

The window at the end of the hall opened onto a balcony which fronted the street and encircled the hotel on three sides. He went to the window.

Cursing under his breath, Blackjack struggled to work his bulky frame through the window, onto the balcony, and into the driving rain.

The window to room seven was open a crack to admit the night breeze. Blackjack eased it on up to allow himself a clear shot. He could make out the silhouetted form of Jack Dancer as he lay sleeping in the bed.

Blackjack braced his gun arm on the sill and took careful aim. He pulled the hammer to full cock.

Suddenly the sky above Tascosa exploded with nature's fury into brilliant sheets of lightning, bathing the balcony in a blinding white light. An ear-shattering cannonade rattled the windows of the hotel.

Blackjack ducked below the sill and hugged the wall, his heart beating rapidly. As the rumbling roll of thunder eased and died away, he raised himself again and resumed his firing position.

Dancer was gone!

Jack came up suddenly on the other side of the bed with his Colt in his hand. The thunder of guns and the lightning fire of sudden death filled the stormy night as both men fired.

The .44 slug left a neat black hole in Blackjack Daniel's forehead. The big man flew crashing through rain-filled space and landed with a splashing, shuddering impact in the muddy street.

Jack moved to the window. He looked down on the massive buckskin-covered mound lying wet and glistening in the quagmire below. He flipped a spent cartridge casing out the open window, replacing it with a fresh bullet. Pushing the window shut and turning back into the room, he shook his head. Then young Jack Dancer went back to bed.

"That was good shooting, Jack," Houston said.

"Doesn't pleasure me any," he replied. "I didn't have time *not* to kill him."

Jack and John Dancer, Temple Houston, Bat Masterson, and Sheriff Willingham had gathered in the undertaker's back room to view the result of Jack's shootout the previous night.

"I'll be damned! That's Phineas Blackwater," John said, bending over the bulbous body in buckskin.

Masterson leaned forward for a closer look, then shook his head.

"That's not his name."

"Huh?"

"Man's name's not Blackwater," Bat told them. "That's Blackjack Daniels . . . or was.

"He was at Adobe Walls when me and some other buffalo hunters had that little set-to with that whole mess of Comanch', back about ten years ago."

Sheriff Willingham turned to the Dancers.

"How'd you boys come to know this hombre?"

"We had us a run-in with him and another man, down on the Red River," Jack told him. "It was my bullet put that hole in his shoulder. Must have been lookin' to even the score."

"I don't think that's why he was here, Jack, and I don't think us meetin' one another on the Red was happenstance, either," John Dancer said. "I believe this man was sent . . . sent to kill you, and me!"

"Even if we knew which way they lit out, there'd be no way to pick up their trail after that gullywasher last night."

John spilled hot coffee into his saucer and blew to cool it. He lifted the saucer to his lips and slurped loudly.

"They'll float to the surface sooner or later, like rotten fish."

"You saying we should just give up lookin'?" Jack asked, looking perplexed.

"I'm saying we should wait . . . 'til we hear some word. No sense runnin' around chasin' our own tails like a couple of wormy hound dogs."

"John, John Dancer."

A wiry little man in a big, wide hat was rushing through the crowded dining hall toward their table. He had the sandblasted look of a man that found little comfort under a roof. His face seemed to have been chiseled from mesa rock, and it was crisscrossed with the fissures of a life lived in sun and wind.

"Tumbleweed Gaines, you old coot. What dust devil blew you to these parts?"

He joined them at the table. John motioned for the waiter to bring another cup, then introduced him to Jack.

"Tumbleweed here is the orneriest old horse apple I ever shared a fire with. Me 'n him have forked more than our share of wild mustangs together, and tore up more saloons."

Jack offered his hand, saying, "Mister Gaines, it's a pleasure, sir. I've heard my uncle speak of you."

"It's a durn lie, then, young'un." The gap-grinned Gaines turned to the elder Dancer.

"It's pure-dee luck I happened on to you, John. I got a wild herd of broomtails spotted over near Taos, with some of the finest horseflesh runnin' in it that I've seen in many a year. Eighty to a hundred head. But I need some help chasin' and corralin' the varmints. How 'bout it? There's some money to be made. The army up at Fort Union will likely take the whole batch after we bust the kinks out of 'em."

John looked at Jack.

"What do you think, partner? We could sure use the money. And I've about had my fill of towns and hotels for a spell."

Jack could see the excitement in his uncle's eyes and knew that John wanted to go.

"Why don't you and Tumbleweed go chase 'em, John. I figure on wandering around some a while yet. See some country."

"Up Colorado way, maybe?"

Jack nodded. "I hear it's pretty country."

"Yep, and big. Most of it straight up and down. It's not likely you'll run on to the McCabes, boy, but I can see you got your mind set.

"Tell you what. I'll chouse down those mustangs with ol' Tumbleweed here and get 'em sold, then head on up there and join you. I'll give you the name of a man I know up in Denver. You can leave word with him where you're at."

They packed up their gear and said their goodbyes, sharing the mutual respect of one strong man for another.

Jack sat the broad back of the buckskin, watching as John Dancer and Tumbleweed Gaines disappeared into a morning haze that hung like a gray, fuzzy blanket on the prairie.

He turned the big horse's nose into the north wind and jabbed his heels into its sides, starting at a trot toward an unknown land and an uncertain future. Suddenly, Jack Dancer felt very much alone.

Chapter Twelve

The weeks that followed pulled Jack Dancer ever nearer the distant purple peaks of the mighty mountains that divide the continent and direct the flow of its waters east or west in their rush to join the vast Atlantic and Pacific oceans. Jack worked his way across the windworn plains of Eastern Colorado, breaking horses, mending fences or clearing land on ranches and farms, sometimes for pay, often for a few hot meals and a dry bunk in the hay.

There was a bite in the autumn air by the time Jack reached the foothills of the Rockies, and the quaking aspen had donned their cloaks of gold. He wandered along the high ridges and into the secluded valleys of the San Juan and Sawatch ranges, always alert, ever searching for the ruthless men who had attacked his peaceful world with gun and chain and had left it in a bloody shambles.

At Telluride, a raw and rugged mining town on the steep slopes of the San Juans, Jack took a job as a wagon guard, riding shotgun on shipments of milled gold and silver ores from the mines of the area to the processors in Denver.

Telluride was a bustling, boisterous, brawling town, with an air of frantic immediacy that was foreign to Jack. He

111

walked among sullen, burly miners in hard hats, Cousin Jacks with defiance in their eyes, fancy-suited millionaires counting stacks of dollars in their heads. He saw the con men and fast buck artists, ruffians and muggers, gamblers and prostitutes—all rushing toward some unseen goal, and not a smile to be seen in the lot. Jack sensed an evil here that he had not known before. The trail towns of Kansas, the cow camps of Texas, Hogtown, Mobeetie—they could be dangerous, rough-and-tumble spots, to be sure. But there had been a sort of code in those places that was missing here. A sense of fair play and a passing acquaintance with decency, that these people did not seem to possess.

Even the violence took a different tack in Telluride. They fought their battles with knotted fist and cleated boot, with brass knuckles, single jacks and knives. When blood ran hot and tempers flared, men rarely face their enemies over smoking six-guns. The bloodied bodies of murdered men were found instead in dark alleys, with stab wounds or bullet holes in their backs. Only the ladies of the night were the same, with love painted on their faces and smiles frozen on their lips.

On his third run out of Telluride, Jack was sitting the shotgun seat of the first wagon in a line of three. An early blast of arctic wind was driving a cutting shower of sleet into the faces of drivers and guards, and the men had their heads pulled down into the sheepskin collars of their coats, like frightened tortoises. Suddenly the wagon lurched and skidded to a halt, almost hurling Jack off the seat and onto the backs of the six-mule team.

"Tree across the road," the muleskinner shouted into the wind. "I'll check it out. You stay up there and keep your eye peeled for trouble."

As the driver's booted foot hit the hub of the wagon wheel on his way to the ground, a half dozen masked renegades rushed from the rocks on either side of the trail, brandishing rifles and six-guns.

"Down off them wagons," one of the highwaymen shouted, "this is a—"

The blast from one barrel of Jack's ten-gauge cut short the outlaw's demand as the charge of buckshot drove him back into the rocks from which he had come. Jack dropped into the well of the wagon beneath the seat and unleashed the other barrel, downing a second robber as he turned to flee. Bullets whined around his head and thudded into the wood planking of the heavy wagon as Jack unlimbered his Colt, firing rapidly. By then the guards from the other two wagons were rushing to join the fray. By the time the shooting had ceased and the wind had cleared the scene of gunsmoke, three men lay dead on the ground, another lay dying, and the remaining two bandits had fled into the forest, one of them dragging a leg and leaving behind a bright, spotted trail of blood. Jack climbed down from the tall wagon and hurried to the edge of the trees, where he stood bent for several minutes, retching and throwing up his heels.

Word of Jack Dancer's gun skills spread rapidly. Six days after the shooting on the trail, he was leaning over a big bowl of stew in Mother Simple's Cafe when he was approached by a tall, angular gentleman in a black frock coat and a Texas-wide hat.

"Jack Dancer?"

Jack looked up into a pair of smiling green eyes set above a prominent, oft-broken nose in a pale, blade-thin face paved with large brown freckles. The man's hair was roan red, hanging to his shoulders. He was clean shaven. He had an affable appearance, but there was that about him, too, that spoke of a confident strength and toughness. Jack took an immediate liking to him.

"Yes, sir, I'm Dancer."

"Samuel Coffee," he said, extending a slender hand. Jack took it.

"Sit down, Mister Coffee," Jack said, pulling out a chair with his left hand. "What can I do for you?"

"It's *Marshal* Coffee, of Ouray, northeast of here."

Jack looked at the smooth cut of the man's coat and vest, unadorned by the glint of official metal.

"How come you don't wear a badge?"

"Same reason I don't wear a paper target pinned to my back." He smiled as he said it. "You kin to John Dancer?"

Jack nodded. "He's my uncle."

"Gun savvy must run in the family, I reckon," the marshal said.

"He taught me some of what he knows. What do you want, Marshal?"

"You ever thought of becoming a lawman, Dancer?"

"Not when I was sober."

"Ha. I like that. Can't say I blame you much, neither," the marshal said. "But that's why I rode over here. I need me a deputy. The job's yours if you'll have it. Forty a month. There's a room and a cot in the jail that goes with the job."

"I don't know anything about being a lawman, sir."

"Not much to know. I just point my finger and say sic 'em. You are a good man with a gun, Dancer. Me, I'm a ringtail terror in a brawl or a free-for-all, and a fair hand with a rifle, but you could curry a good-sized horse in the time it takes me to get a gun out of a holster. How 'bout it?"

"I appreciate the offer, Marshal, but I'm in Colorado to find some men I followed up from Texas. When I get word on where they might be, I'm gone."

"Fair enough. I wouldn't try to hold you. You might as well be doing me some good in the meantime, though. Besides, if these men you're after should run afoul of the law, what better place to hear about it than a marshal's office, right?"

"I reckon so, but . . ."

"But what?"

"Nothin, I guess. Alright, I'll give it a try—for a while."

Marshal Coffee settled in the straight-back chair as a satisfied smile started at the corners of his mouth and spread to his lively eyes.

A large, husky woman in an apron stopped at the lawman's elbow, asking if he would care for a cup of coffee. The lawman flinched noticeably when he looked up into the waitress' mannish, pock-marked face. His expression softened again and he held up a palm in polite refusal.

"No thank you, lovely lady. When he finishes his stew, I am going to buy Deputy Dancer here a drink."

Gunter McCabe rubbed a spot of frost off the inside of the window pane with a rapid circular motion of his fingers and peeped out into the white-blanketed landscape in front of the cabin. Even filtered through the dark smoked lenses of his spectacles, the brilliant reflection of the sun attacked his sensitive eyes and set them to watering. He jerked his head back from the window and clapped his hands over his face.

"Dadgum it! Avery, you come look. I can't see a stinkin' thing for the glare off that snow."

Avery pushed himself off the bunk against the chinked log wall and shuffled to the window. "Pink-eyed freak," he mumbled under his breath. He wiped at the circular peep hole again with his own hand and peered outside.

"Yeah, here he comes."

"About time," Oran grumbled from his seat at a rustic table. He was playing solitaire with a dog-eared deck of cards and a marked lack of enthusiasm. He was cheating, but still unable to win.

The rough plank door of the cabin was thrust open as Cash burst in, bringing with him a frigid blast of air as an uninvited guest. He stomped his feet and rubbed his gloved hands together.

"Brrr. Colder than a spinster's prospects."

"Shut that dadgum door," Oran shouted. He gave his brother an impatient scowl. "Where's my tobacco?"

"Still on the horse. Get it yourself."

Oran stood to his full six-foot-four height, knocking the chair backward to the hard-packed dirt floor as he got to his feet. He balled his fingers into a fist as big as a Virginia ham and started toward his younger brother.

"I'll get it, I'll get it," Cash said. "Just let me get warm first. Besides, I got some news for you. I got us a job."

"A *job?"* Gunter sat up with a start.

"Don't get shook, Gunter. It ain't work, or anything so vile or disgusting as that. Ol' Dad would turn over in his grave if any of us was to lift a finger in honest labor.

"Naw," Cash continued, "this is easy money. This little gal I was with last night in Denver told me about this customer of hers, an old prospector that lives in a raw board shack on his claim, right around the mountain from here. Wears a money belt it'd take three men and a boy to lift. All we got to do is ride over there and take it off him. Old geezer lives all by hisself. I rode by there on my way in."

Avery jumped off the bunk and rushed to face his brother. There was a look of incredulity on his face.

"You serious, Cash? My lord, man, we can't do that. We aren't criminals!"

"Oh no? Then you ride back down to Texas and tell that to the Rangers. Maybe they'll lift the warrants on us. That ten thousand ol' Dad sent us before he went and got hisself murdered isn't going to last forever, you know. You seen the letter from Carter Bozeman. The state of Texas has attached everything this family ever had. We can't touch a penny of it as long as we're wanted by the law. Dad should never have had that slob Daniels kill them Dancers. Now they got us for murder."

"We didn't do it," Avery insisted.

"I know that, and you know it. But the everlovin' Texas Rangers don't know it. They got it figured Tom Dancer died of the beating we gave him."

"We? What we? That was you, Cash."

"You seen the wanted poster Carter sent us, Avery. Your name—Oran's and Gunter's too—is right there with mine. All the same size type. All of us wanted for murder. We got to face it. Dad's money and everything else that figured to be ours is gone to us. We are poor little orphans, boys. We got to do for ourselves now. This country is full of gold and silver in the pockets of weaker men. We just got to have the courage to take it from them. Now, you with me on this or not? 'Cause if you ain't, I'm going it alone."

Cash's brothers were silent for a moment, then Gunter spoke up.

"I don't see we've got any other choice. What do you think, Oran? You're the oldest."

Oran walked over to Cash and put his massive arm across his shoulders.

"Cash, here, is the smartest of us. We all know that, I reckon. I figure he's the one to call the shots."

"I don't like it," Avery said. "What if the old guy puts the law on us?"

"Avery, you ain't even *half*-witted. He won't be alive to do nothing. Whatever we do from here on out, we can't leave any witness. Agreed?"

They all nodded, though somewhat tentatively, as their sudden shift in lifestyle and moral direction was slow to take hold.

The issue apparently decided to his satisfaction, Cash

began to peel off his heavy coat. Oran wrapped a meaty
fist around his arm, halting him.

"I said you was the smartest, little brother. I am the big-
gest. Before you shuck that coat, you go back outside, tend
your horse and get my tobacco."

Jack pulled the tattered sheet of notepaper from under
his pillow and turned up the wick of the lamp beside the
cot. No matter how many times he read the letter from his
Uncle John, it always revealed the same shocking truth.

> *My dear Jack,*
>   *I take pen in hand with a heavy heart, for it falls
> on me to give you the worst possible news. Your ma
> and your brother Tom are dead . . .*

He colored slightly when he saw the inky blotches his
tears had created the first time he had read it. He would be
eighteen come April, a grown man. Too old to cry.

The news had not come as a total surprise, really, for he
had long since been haunted by a feeling that his family
was dead. It had first occurred to him that stormy night in
Hogtown, when he had looked down onto the rain- and
mud-splattered body of Blackjack Daniels, lying in the
street below his window. Nonetheless, he had cried when
he saw it confirmed in writing. Cried for the good times
lost, rather than for the dead. Cried for what might have
been.

Jack returned his attention to the letter in his hand.

> *Their bodies were found by a lady come to claim her
> laundry, and they had been dead a spell.*
>   *The official version is that Tom passed of his inju-
> ries, and that your ma keeled over upon finding him
> dead. Doc Hackett ain't so sure, however. He says*

they could of been suffocated somehow, the both of them. I see the hand of Dad McCabe in this, but that is something we might never know, for he is dead too.

You recall that Mr. Fish that was with Blackwater or Blackjack—whichever—on that whiskey wagon? Well, Carter Bozeman and a couple other of McCabe's cronies come on him going through that big house of old Dad's, picking up everthing of value he could lay a hand to. And Dad McCabe was laying dead in his study.

Fish told them the old man had refused him payment for a job of work he'd done for him (most likely for his part in that business up on the Red). So he shot the old skinflint right between the eyes with that little toy gun of his. Mister Fish is not with us anymore, neither. They hung him from the second story balcony of the house.

How I come to know of this, Jack, is I came back this way to check on your folks after Tumbleweed and me had sold off them horses we caught. Got a tolerable price, too. Anyhow, I saw they was buried proper, beside Big Jack.

You know that me and Tom was close. We grew up together and fought together in the war. He was a good man, Tom was, and he thought the world of you. Always tried to do right by you. It would pleasure me if you would try to think of him like he was when you were growing up and not like he had gotten the last time you seen him. Your ma never taken to me much, but she was a good woman too, in her way.

I will send this letter to Johnny Latigo in Denver in hopes you have got in touch with him, and if all goes well, partner, I will be up to join you in the spring.

Your friend and only living relative,
John Dancer

Checking his pocket watch, Jack saw that it was time for
his rounds. He folded the letter and put it back under his
pillow, then swung his long legs off the cot and blew out
the lamp. He stepped under his hat and strapped his gun
belt around his waist. He paused for a glance in the oval
mirror propped against the wall on top of a three-drawer
chest. The image staring back at him had changed consid-
erably since Buffalo Springs. He was no longer a skinny
farm boy in too small overalls. He was deeper in the chest
now, his arms heavier, his legs stouter, his stomach flat and
hard as hickory wood. Part of the change was due to his
having attained his natural growth, but mostly he had been
toughened by the trails he had ridden and the trials he had
known. His mustache was full and neatly trimmed, his jaws
scraped clean. He had gained an inner strength too. He was
tough-minded. Confident. Not full of himself, but comfortable with who he was and what he was today. He straightened his collar, pulled on his heavy coat and gloves, and
turned to the door.

It was an uncommonly quiet night in Ouray. The sudden
drop in temperature had driven the usual rowdy bands of
revelers indoors to hover around the glowing red bellies of
iron stoves, and had put a temporary restraint on their buoy-
ant moods and rough manners. After a few days, when they
had adjusted to the change in season and become bored
with sedentary pleasures, they would venture forth again to
wreak havoc upon the town and restore its streets to normal
battlefield conditions.

Jack trotted toward two men who were rolling and grap-
pling in the hard-frozen, snow-dusted street, throwing
mitten-padded punches harmlessly into heavy parkas.

"Hey! You fellows stop that nonsense and get yourselves
in out of the cold."

The polluted participants clambered to their feet and retreated through the nearest saloon door, secretly grateful

for the excuse the lawman had supplied them to escape the bitter weather.

He had finished his rounds and was headed back for the jail. As he passed Casey's Silver Summit Saloon, a semi-ambulatory patron stumbled out the door and headed for the street, walking at an impossible forward tilt. The edge of the boardwalk ambushed the tipsy traveler and he fell headlong onto the frozen, rutted turf. Jack walked over and hefted the wilted drunk to his feet, threw a shoulder under one arm and hauled him off to the jail.

"Can't sleep there on the ground, old timer. You'd be froze solid before sunup."

Deputy Marshal Jack Dancer had no inkling at that moment how that small act of compassion would alter his life.

Chapter Thirteen

"**J**ump me."

Jack made the required move, taking his opponent's man. Charlie Tenkiller cackled gleefully as he moved his red king, hopping square to square to decimate the Deputy's black forces.

"You are too much for me, Charlie," Jack said, and leaned back away from the checkerboard between them. "That's six straight you've whomped me."

His opponent in the game was seated on the edge of a bunk in one of the cells, leaning over a game board that had been placed on an upended whiskey crate. Jack sat opposite him on a short three-legged stool.

Charlie was a short, stocky, wisecracking half-breed Cherokee—the drunk that Jack had carried to the jail the previous night. He worked a small, unproductive claim back in the hills behind Ouray on the slopes of Red Cloud Peak. When the cold snap had hit, Charlie shut down his operation for the winter and came to town to get drunk. Judging by his red-rimmed eyes, skinned nose and slack features on this morning after, he had succeeded brilliantly.

When Charlie woke up in the cell that morning, he felt

122

like someone had used his bottom jaw to scoop out the
stables. He had launched into a vituperative dialogue
against the whole premise of law enforcement, in the Cherokee tongue. When Jack responded in the same language,
Charlie was delighted. From that point on, they had become
kindred spirits and bosom friends.

"One more game?" Charlie asked.

"I don't think so," said Jack. "How about I buy you
breakfast instead?"

At that moment, an icy draft on the back of his neck
alerted Jack to the opening of the office door. He unwound
off the low stool and started for the front room. When he
reached the door that separated the cell area from the office,
he was almost bowled over by a small figure bundled in a
fur coat barreling through.

"What have you done with my father?"

Jack's jaw went slack as he found himself staring at the
most beautiful girl he had ever set eyes on. She was young,
maybe younger than he was himself. Her long, straight hair
was strikingly black and sprinkled with melted snowflakes
that sparkled in the lamplight like diamonds in a crown.
Her eyes were wide and clear, a mile deep, and almost as
black as her hair. Her full lips had a slight pout about them,
and she had smooth, tan skin the color of dark honey. Small
pointed boots extended below the bulky fur wrap that
threatened to drag the floor. She was an Indian Princess in
sensible shoes.

"Did you hear what I asked you, Marshal?"

"Huh? Oh, no ma'am. I'm not the marshal. I am his
deputy."

The girl spotted Charlie, peeking his head around the
bars of the open cell door. She rushed to him.

"Daddy. Must I hogtie you to keep you out of trouble?"

Then she noticed the skinned nose and the scab on his

chin. She turned back to Jack with her black eyes flashing blue fire.

"You brute! You *beat* him? Why aren't you out arresting real criminals instead of brutalizing poor innocents like my father?"

"No, ma'am, I . . ."

"How much is his bail? I want him released immediately into my custody—this instant. Do you hear me?"

Charlie jumped in. "Hold on, Laura. Leave the poor boy his scalp. He never done nothin' to me, except maybe save my life. I skint my nose fallin' down. Passed out. He drug me in here so's I wouldn't freeze."

"And he is not under arrest, ma'am. The cell door's not even been locked. He is free to go, anytime."

The girl was embarrassed and tried to sink down inside the fuzzy collar of her wolfskin coat. She shrugged her shoulders and looked at Jack.

"I'm sorry. Daddy calls me his 'wild Indian,' and I guess maybe I am a bit too eager to take to the warpath. Want to sign a peace treaty, white man?"

"No need, I surrender. I just offered to buy Charlie's breakfast. Will you join us, ma'am?"

"Not ma'am. Laura. I'm sorry, I can't. I have to get to my job. I work in the kitchen at the Uncompahgre House. But I'll feed you dinner tonight, at our house. Will you come?"

He did come, that evening and every night for a week. Jack had never been at ease around girls, but it was different with Laura. He caught himself chattering on, telling her things he never thought he would share with anyone. He told her of the shooting in Buffalo Springs and how he had joined up with the trail drive. About his trouble with Harvey, and of his run-in with the Comanche, and how frightened he had been. In a week's time she knew about John Dancer, the McCabes, Blackjack Daniels, Temple

Houston, Hogtown and Mobeetie, Charles Goodnight, and the Palo Duro Canyon. And she came to know what had happened to Tom and his mother. All Jack knew was that he was root and branch, full bore, whole-hog in love.

Jack had developed a sudden, inordinate interest in the game of checkers. Any evening he was off duty would find him at the table in the Tenkiller kitchen, bent over a checkerboard across from Charlie. After a few games, which Charlie generally won, the old Indian would demonstrate the wisdom of his forebears, yawn sleepily, and retire to his room, leaving the young people alone. Jack and Laura would then sit before the fire and visit. Sometimes she would read to him from a book of poetry she favored, and Jack would pretend to be interested. He loved the sweet, throaty sound of her voice and the way the expressions on her face changed during the reading of the lyrical passages. But mostly, they just talked.

Laura worked to support her father's dream. His gold mine in the sky. Her small salary kept the larder filled in their modest home. But she met each day with a happy heart, not minding the work. She loved Charlie Tenkiller just the way he was. Jack was busy too, but the young couple found the time to be together.

When the deep snows came, they went on moonlight sleigh rides along the rim of the forest outside town, huddled together under a blanket for warmth and for pleasure. They took long walks in the crisp, clear air, and sat in sheltered bowers among the evergreens.

On the night that it happened, they were reclining, hand in hand, before the fireplace. Laura was quiet, intent on the dancing, crackling blaze that was eagerly devouring the pine logs. Jack turned on his side to gain a better view of her as his eyes traveled the length of her lithe, willowy body. Summoning his courage, he bent to kiss her. She greeted him with parted lips. Her hand went to the back of his neck and she urged him closer. Jack kissed her gently, but passionately, at the smooth base of her neck, on the lobes of her ears, on her closed eyelids. Laura moaned. Her breathing became hoarse and heavy. "Jack, oh Jack . . . I love you. I love you."

Panting with passion, Jack became suddenly aware of his excited state and of the insistent throbbing of the blood in his veins. Pulling abruptly away he sat upright, swiping at his eyes and face with his palm. Then he turned to face Laura, who lay heavy-lidded and flushed.

"Laura . . . I'm sorry. I forgot myself. Forgive me."

She smiled, sitting up slowly.

"There's nothing to forgive. I think I started it." Then, squeezing his hand, she whispered, "But I'll not apologize."

They sat for a long time in remembered propriety, Laura leaning back against his chest, his arms cradling her, the fingers of their hands intertwined. Snowflakes as big as dollars drifted past the window as the fire in the hearth sent playful orange reflections onto the pane.

"There's a mess of boxes and crates in that little store-room needs to be gone through," Sam Coffee said. "Old papers, warrants and such. Most of it trash. Get rid of anything don't look like it needs keepin', will you?"

"You going to help?" Jack asked the marshal.

"That's why we call you *deputy,*" Sam said, a big grin lighting his freckled features. He evacuated the chair behind the desk and strapped on his sidearm.

"I'll check on you later, Deputy," Coffee said, rubbing it in. "I got me some marshalin' to do."

He wrestled himself into a heavy overcoat, grabbed a rifle off the wall rack by the door, and plunged outside. Jack watched him go, then allowed himself a grin of his own. *Marshal away, Sam,* he thought. *I'm not the one out there tromping around in snow to my knees.*

He went to the storeroom and hauled an armload of boxes back to the office, placing them in a stack near the pot-bellied stove in the center of the room. He pulled over a chair, poured himself a cup of coffee, then sat down to his assigned chore.

Jack had always imagined that being a law dog would be an exciting, romantic, action-packed way of life, but he was discovering that it was more a matter of serving as combination paper shuffler, nursemaid to drunks, and night watchman—even in a frontier town as unruly and unkempt as Ouray. With a sigh he opened the first box. He sifted through the dusty, yellowed reams of notices, warrants, documents, and dodgers one at a time, shuttling the majority of them into the open door of the iron stove at his right hand. Suddenly he stopped short, staring at the aging wanted poster he had uncovered.

WANTED FOR MURDER
CHARLES H. TENKILLER
ALSO KNOWN AS
CHEROKEE CHARLIE

The smaller type at the bottom of the sheet explained that the fugitive had savagely murdered two white men, Benjamin A. Wenzel and Ezekial "Zeke" Eastwood, on or about June 6, 1869, near the town of Tahlequah, Indian Territory. Any information regarding the whereabouts of said fugitive was to be directed to the U. S. District Court in Fort Smith, Arkansas.

Jack sat motionless, stunned into inactivity, for several minutes. Then he folded the poster and pushed it into the depths of his pants pocket. He filled his arms with the remaining papers in the box, stuffed them into the fire and slapped shut the stove door. He threw on his coat and rushed from the office, headed for the Uncompahgre House.

He rapped at the kitchen entrance to the hotel. Shortly, the door opened a crack and a tall, Negro gentleman in a white apron peered out through the slit.

"Morning, Deputy. Something I can do for you, sir?"

"Sorry to bother you," Jack said, "but I need to speak with Miss Tenkiller for a moment."

The door closed. In a few seconds it reopened and Laura came out with her wrap around her shoulders.

"Jack, what's wrong? Has something happened to Daddy?"

He shook his head and ushered her away from the building with a hand on her elbow.

"I need to talk to you. Can you take a few minutes?"

She nodded and he led her to a small cafe across the street. When they were seated with steaming cups before them—tea for her, coffee for him—Jack dug into his pocket and withdrew the poster. He unfolded it and handed it across the table.

Laura stared at the fading dodger for a long time, then looked at Jack, her gaze steady.

"Well?" Jack said.

"Well, what?"

"Did you know about this?"

"Of course I knew about it. That is why I was so upset to find Daddy in jail that day we met. I was afraid someone would remember this old charge."

"Is it true?" he asked.

She nodded. "As far as it goes. He killed those men, yes. This—"

Laura Tenkiller looked at the broadside in her hand as if touching it had defiled her.

"This thing doesn't tell why he did it. Are you going to arrest my daddy?"

Jack reached across to retrieve the poster, putting it into

his vest pocket. Then he laid his hand atop hers and gave it a squeeze.

"Of course not. But I want to know what happened."

Laura took a sip of her tea, stalling for time, loathe to recall the ugly memories. Then, gathering herself, she told him that she and her mother, a full-blooded Cherokee woman, had been alone in the house the night the two men, Eastwood and Wenzel, came to the door. Laura was three years old at the time. Charlie had been off on a trip buying horses, and her mother refused the men entry. They had been drinking, and they became loud and abusive. Her mother had shut the door in their faces and locked it.

"About an hour later," Laura recalled, "they came back, drunker than before. They pounded and kicked on the door until they broke through. Then they dragged Mama off, screaming, into the bedroom and shut the door.

"I stood at the door, crying and afraid, while they . . . did what they came for. I wasn't tall enough to reach and turn the knob. I could hear my mother screaming, sobbing, begging. Then the screaming stopped, and all I could hear were ugly grunts and squeaking bed springs."

When the men were done and the noises from the other room had ceased, Laura told him, the door opened. The intruders stepped over the crouched, cowering form of the girl and stumbled, laughing, into the night.

"I ran to my parents' bed and crawled up beside my mother. I tried to wake her, but she was dead."

Jack heard that, when Charlie returned, late the next evening, he found his daughter sitting on the bed beside her mother's battered, lifeless body, her tiny face tear-streaked, her wide, black eyes filled with horror. His wife had been ravaged and strangled.

Laura had told her father, as best she could for a child so young, what had happened. Charlie Tenkiller took the child with him on a tour of area saloons and other gathering places until, finally, they located the men. Laura had identified them, and the men had smugly and laughingly admitted to their foul crime, saying, "She was nothing but a damn squaw, nohow." Though filled with rage, Charlie had not attacked his wife's killers that night. He left Laura with friends and went into Tahlequah to report the crime.

The Cherokee tribal police grimly explained to the grief-stricken husband that they had been granted no authority to arrest a white man, no matter what accusations might be brought against him, unless they caught him in the act of committing a crime. Then they could only transport him to white authorities for mediation. The native force's legal jurisdiction was limited to making the savage Indians of the territory abide by the white man's rules.

"Daddy still didn't take the law into his own hands. He rode to Fort Smith, in Arkansas, to lodge a complaint with the U. S. Marshals office there. They agreed that the murder of a squaw was a crime, and likely should be punished, but refused to take action, they said, because it would be a waste of taxpayer's dollars to bring the killers to trial, for no jury of white men would convict one of their own for any crime against an Indian.

"Daddy broke then. When he got back, he found those two in a saloon, waited for them to come outside, and he killed them with a hunting knife . . . then he scalped them. Afterward, he gathered me up, along with a few belongings, and we ran. We've been running ever since."

Tears were streaming down Laura's cheeks, crystal remembrances of grief and fear. Jack moved beside her to comfort her.

"Don't say anything to anyone, Laura, not even to Charlie. I'll contact Temple Houston. Maybe he can help us clear this up."

Chapter Fourteen

"Morning, Jack."

"Morning, Miz Coffee. Sam's not here. He had to ride over to Telluride to pick up some papers."

Jack liked the marshal's wife. She was a little slip of a woman, not pretty, but with a smile that could light up a room. She spoke with a soft, Southern accent that was lyrical.

"I know. He had me up cookin' eggs and side meat before the cock crowed. Is that ornery husband of mine treatin' you alright?"

He nodded and smiled.

"Jack, this may be none of my business, but aren't you sparkin' that little Tenkiller girl?"

Jack blushed and stammered a bit. "I'm right fond of Laura, yes'm."

"Thought so," she said. "That's why I was so surprised to see her and her pa getting on the early stage. Looked like they were taking everything they owned along with 'em."

"What?" Jack jumped to his feet. "You sure, Miz Coffee?"

131

She assured him that she was certain. Jack excused himself and bolted from the office into the street, not taking the time to put on a coat or hat. Mary Ruth Coffee watched him hurrying away. She shook her head sadly.

He ran recklessly down the frozen, deeply-rutted street, brushing past curious, bundled-up pedestrians to the Tenkiller home. He cleared the fence at the edge of the yard without slowing, bounded onto the porch and burst through the front door.

"Laura!"

Jack rushed room to room, hoping to find something that would indicate that Laura and Charlie Tenkiller had merely gone on a short trip, or that they were not gone at all. All the clothing was missing from Laura's closet. The drawers of her clothes chest stood open and empty. A bright rectangle on the papered wall, where her mother's picture had been hanging, jumped out at him from its faded surroundings, mocking his urgent search.

His heart sinking, Jack returned to the front room. The furniture was all that remained in the Tenkiller home. All their personal belongings had been stripped from the house. He slumped onto the settee, stunned and disbelieving, trying to think. The emptiness of the abandoned dwelling swept in on him like a wind off a frozen lake, chilling him.

This could not be happening. It must be a cruel hoax of some sort. He noticed an envelope tacked to the mantle over the fireplace. He jumped to his feet and snatched it loose. It was addressed simply to Jack Dancer. With trembling fingers he tore away the envelope and opened the folded note.

My dearest Jack,

This is the most difficult thing I have ever had to do.

Daddy and I are leaving Ouray, as we have left so

*many other places. Your finding of that old poster con-
vinced me that we are not yet far enough removed, in
time or distance, from that awful mess in the Indian
Nations.*

*I know, my darling, that you would never endanger
my father, but I do not have the right to assume that
someone else may not. And so, we must leave.*

*Please don't blame Daddy. He is leaving only at my
insistence. He is aware of how I feel toward you and
was willing to stay, and to risk his personal safety for
my sake and for yours, but I could not allow it.*

*I love you, Jack. I shall always love you and trea-
sure the memories of our time together. But I must beg
you not to try to find us. You will be ever in my
thoughts and dreams. Be happy, my love, and good-
bye.*

Laura

Mrs. Coffee had said they left on the early stage. That
was nearly four hours ago. He rushed from the house and
down the street to the stage depot.

"Yes sir, Deputy, left right on schedule," the agent assured him. "Bound first for Telluride, then east to Denver.
Anythin' wrong?"

Jack turned and walked back to the office. His heart was
a lead weight in his chest.

"Whew-ee! It's colder than a banker's heart."

Marshal Sam Coffee hung his coat on a peg by the door
and crossed to the glowing stove, stamping his feet and
blowing into cupped hands. He turned his back to the fire
and stuck his fingers in his hind pockets.

"Evening, Jack. Everything quiet?"

Jack said nothing.

"Jack . . . something wrong, son?"

"I'll be leaving, Sam."

"Yeah, I was afraid of that," Coffee said with a sigh. "You've heard, then?"

"Huh? Heard what?"

"They are fixing to hang one of your McCabe brothers up in Fort Collins. Oran McCabe. Killed a prospector up that way, over a stake that didn't amount to twenty dollars."

Marshal Coffee walked to pull a folded newspaper from his coat pocket and waved it in Jack's direction.

Jack lurched to snatch the paper out of the marshal's fingers.

"Lower right hand corner, front page," Coffee directed.

Jack read the small article. Oran McCabe was scheduled to hang the following Saturday at ten o'clock in the morning. He looked up anxiously.

"Any information on the other three?"

"There's nothing in any notice to indicate that they are wanted for crimes in Colorado. Far as I know, they weren't involved."

"They will be," Jack replied.

The McCabes were no-account in Jack's book, but he knew that they were a close family. Cash, Avery, and Gunter would not stand idly by while the law hanged their elder brother. They would try to break Oran out. He was sure of it. And when they did, Jack Dancer would be there, waiting.

"Sam . . . you know I got to go."

The marshal nodded.

"The badge will be waiting for you whenever you want it back. And you take care, Jack. From what you've told me, that's a mighty mean bunch you're fixin' to tangle with. You are just one man. You're good, but the odds are against you.

"I'd go with you if I could, boy."

Jack had intended to follow after Laura and Charlie, but that must wait now. If he was to have a chance at stopping the McCabes, it would be necessary that he ride straight through to Fort Collins.

He hurriedly packed his gear, checked his guns, said goodbye to Sam, then hustled to the livery for his horse. One more stop at the mercantile to pick up the few trail supplies he would need for the trip, and he could be on his way. He wished he had a way of reaching John, but he had no notion as to where his uncle might be at the moment. If time allowed, he would stop and check with that Mister Latigo in Denver.

Heading out, Jack pushed his horse past the empty Ten-killer house. It looked forlorn and lonely in the dimness of approaching dusk. A lump welled in his throat, and he wondered if he would ever see Laura again. No way to tell what the future would hold, not from where he sat his saddle today. His thoughts drifted back, too, to the last time he had seen his brother Tom, with drool running off his chin. And to the cold, defeated attitude his mother had displayed when she told him that she did not want him there anymore. He patted his horse's neck and turned his eyes to the long trail ahead.

"Has it just come down on me, old friend, or is life this cruel to one and all?"

"You expect a man to eat this mess? I've seen hogs slopped with better grub."

Oran McCabe picked at the lumpy offering piled on the tin plate he was holding and glowered through the bars at the scarecrow pinned to the deputy's badge.

"Hogs got a future. Don't you worry about it, McCabe. You don't have time left to starve."

The jailer smiled at the prisoner, exposing a mouthful of long, yellow teeth canted in a dozen directions. Oran thought they looked like dominoes in a row, about to fall.

"You're a loony-looking jackass," Oran said, "and stupid to boot."

"That may be, but I ain't the one locked up in there, waitin' for a noose."

The deputy showed him another golden grin, then left the cell area, shutting the heavy wooden door behind him.

"Hey, friend." It was the prisoner in the cell adjoining Oran's, brought in the night before for beating a woman and breaking up a saloon. "If you ain't going to eat that, pass it over here, will ya?"

Oran McCabe raised the tin plate to his nose, sniffed at the food, shrugged his beefy shoulders, and began to eat.

It had been a week since that jury had filed into the courtroom to announce their unanimous verdict. A week since the judge had sentenced him to hang. On Saturday. What day was it now? Tuesday or Wednesday? He had lost count.

Where in blazes were those blasted brothers of his, Oran wondered? Why hadn't they busted him out of this box?

Oran stepped up onto the bunk and grabbed the bars of the high window with both hands. He pulled his eyes level with the sill and peered outside, where he could see the dreadful shadow of the gallows. Then he let himself slide down the wall to the bed. He slumped forward and buried his face in his hands.

Oran McCabe was crying.

"Consarn it, Avery, I never said we weren't going to break him out. I just said it's his own stupid fault he's in this mess."

"How you figger? You're the one said we should take what we want from weaker men, Cash."

"Not in a town with a lawman around every corner, for cryin' out loud," Cash said. "And I said no witnesses. He should have killed the gal the old miner was with too."

Avery shook his head. "It's got awful easy for you to talk of killin', little brother." He walked to stare out the cabin window. "What have we come to? A year ago we were respectable, envied men with the money and the power to do or to be anything we wanted. Now Dad is dead. Murdered. Oran's in jail set to hang. And we three sit here in this decrepit cabin, snapping at one another, talkin' about killin' folks with no more thought than we'd give to wringin' a chicken's neck for Sunday dinner.

"It all started going to pieces when you jumped Tom Dancer in that barn, Cash. You lost your head, beating the man that way. You're out of control. Kill crazy."

"Oran shot the old woman! That's what run us out of Texas . . . and Dad hired Tom and the old lady killed. That's what put us on the hook for murder. It was Jack Dancer started it all when he shot me, not me whippin' up on that one-armed farmer."

The brothers were nose to nose, shouting at each other. Gunter McCabe pulled his gun and fired it into the ceiling.

"Stop it, both of you. Fighting amongst ourselves don't get Oran out of jail," Gunter said. "Avery, you quit your darn whining about what was and what happened. It can't be changed and we're all sick of hearing it. Cash, you are supposed to be the one callin' the shots, so do it. Come up with a plan."

Both men looked at the albino and the anger faded from their faces. Cash nodded.

"You're right, Gunter, and I already been thinkin' on it. Here's what we do . . ."

It was late on a crisp, bright Thursday afternoon when Jack Dancer rode into Fort Collins. He went directly to the sheriff's office. As he entered, the toothy deputy behind the desk started, swung his heels from the desktop to the floor, pushed his hat back off his nose, and sat up straight.

"Howdy," Jack said, "Sheriff in?"

"Ketchum? Nah. Gone to supper. Back directly," the deputy told him. "Who's askin'?"

"Name's Jack Dancer . . . You got Oran McCabe locked up back there?" He motioned with a flat thumb toward the door to the cell area.

"Why? What's your interest?"

Jack noticed that the deputy's right hand had slipped below the desk and come to rest on his leg near his gun. As he started to answer, the office door opened to admit a large, heavy set man. A sheriff's star peeked from behind his open vest. The lawman was graying at the temples and his heavy jowls were host to full, bushy sideburns. Alert blue eyes evaluated the young stranger blocking his path.

Jack extended his hand. "Sheriff Ketchum?"

Ketchum owned up with a nod and accepted Jack's proffered palm with a clean, hard jerk.

"My name is Jack Dancer, sir. I've come with a warning. The man you're fixing to hang on Saturday, Oran McCabe, is one of four brothers. I have a strong notion the others will attempt to break him out of your jail."

"Oh? And how did you come to this realization, Mister Dancer? You know McCabe, do you?"

"I do. Followed them here from Texas. The McCabe family is responsible for the deaths of my mother and brother.

"They are a close bunch, Sheriff Ketchum. They'll not stand by and see one of their own dangling from a rope. They will be duty bound to try to free their brother Oran."

"Dancer, you say. I've heard the name."

"Probably you've heard tell of my uncle, John Dancer. He's known to be good with a gun."

"No. That's not it. Aren't you the young man put down that holdup out of Telluride some months back?"

"I was part of stopping it. I had help. The past few

months, I've been deputy to Marshal Samuel Coffee in Ouray."

The Sheriff shooed the deputy from behind his desk and lowered himself slowly and gingerly into the chair, grimacing as he sat.

"Dang piles will be the death of me. Can't sit a saddle without bawling like a baby." He was voicing his complaint more for his own benefit than for the enlightenment of the other two men in the room.

"I know Coffee, or of him," Ketchum said. "Good man. Well, Dancer, if you've got the straight of it on this jailbreak business, I could use some extra help. You want to wear a deputy badge for a couple days 'til we get McCabe hung and planted? Can't pay you, but I'll buy your supper."

"Hungry as I am right now, Sheriff," Jack said, "you may have a bad bargain. Yes, I reckon I'll sign on with you . . . just until the hanging."

Ketchum muttered an oath of sorts to swear him in, then Jack brought his gear into the jail. He would sleep in one of the cells. The deputy, Morton Fowler, escorted him into the cell area.

Jack stashed his bedroll on a bunk in an empty cell, then walked over to look in on Oran McCabe. He stood a while, staring at the prisoner. Oran fidgeted under his steady gaze.

"What the blazes you gawkin' at?"

"Don't you know me, McCabe?"

The big man leaned forward and squinted at the new jailer. His face paled and his mouth dropped open.

"You! You're supposed to be dead."

"Not likely," Jack said. "Your man wasn't good enough. Not by a long shot."

Chapter Fifteen

Three grim riders emerged from among a jumble of mammoth boulders on the rugged, pine-covered slope overlooking the sleeping town of Fort Collins. A hesitant sun was just beginning to chase the grays and purples from rooftops and streets into the alleys and behind the buildings of the village. The intrusive and arrogant crowing of a rooster could be heard from below as the men shifted nervously in their saddles.

"Let's cover everything again before we go in," Cash said.

"Horsefeathers. We been over it a dozen times."

"Then this'll be one more for good measure, Gunter. I don't want no mistakes. This is no Sunday picnic we're starting out on."

"If it was Sunday," Gunter said with a grin, "it'd be too late for ol' Oran."

"That ain't funny." Avery swung an arm around at his albino brother, missing, but causing Gunter to dodge the blow and slip halfway from the saddle.

"Knock it off, the both of you," Cash snapped. "Oran's waiting.

"Now," he continued, fishing a watch from a vest pocket, "it's quarter to six. The Sheriff don't go on duty until eight or better. That means the deputy will be alone in the jail until then.

"Gunter, you got the livery. Take care of the hostler first off. He's an old buzzard, and crippled to boot. Won't be no problem. Kill him if you need to, but no shooting. Use your knife or a pitchfork or something. Get Oran's horse saddled and out of there, then set the fire. Make certain that it's going good before you leave. Then you circle around and wait in the alley behind the general store. We'll have left our horses there before we go in. When we give you the signal, come a'runnin' with all four of the horses.

"Avery, you take the west side of the jail building. I'll come up on the east. The deputy will likely run out to see what the ruckus is when folks see the barn afire. If he runs to the fire, we let him go and you and me will scoot inside. If he stops on the porch, we'll have him in a crossfire and we drop him."

"What if he don't come out of the jail?" Avery asked. He had said it several times before, and the question came across as if he were reading a line from a play.

"Then we go in after him. I'll saunter in like I was reporting the fire. You wait to the count of ten and bust in, making noise. That'll get his attention off me and I'll kill him. Then we get Oran and we're gone. Gunter, soon as we show at that door—"

"I know," Gunter said, "come a'runnin' with the horses."

"Right. Any questions?"

Avery and Gunter shook him off.

"Let's do it."

Jack woke to the crowing of the rooster. He sat up on the edge of the bunk, stretched, yawned, and scratched himself.

He slipped on his boots and set his hat on the back of his head, then checked his gun and buckled it in place on his hip. He walked out into the corridor fronting the cells.

As he walked toward the office, he noted that Oran McCabe was in his bunk, his broad back turned toward the cell door. Jack went on past and entered the front room. Deputy Fowler was standing before a potbellied stove, watching the coffee pot that was sitting on the stovetop as it spit and sputtered, beginning to boil.

"Coffee's about ready, Dancer. Have a seat."

Jack sat down in a worn ladderback chair and pulled a strip of jerked venison from his inside vest pocket. He picked the lint off the dried meat and popped it into the corner of his mouth.

"If you're right about those McCabes trying to bust their brother out, when you figger they'll hit us?"

"Today. And I suspect it could happen any minute. If it were me, I'd strike early, before there's a lot of folks on the streets. The fewer guns I had to face, the better I'd like it."

The deputy looked concerned. "Reckon we ought to get the sheriff in early?"

Jack smiled. "He is way ahead of both of us, Mort. He is staked out across the street in the assayer's office right now, watching the jail."

Deputy Fowler poured two tin cups full of scalding coffee and handed one to Jack.

"How come he didn't tell me? Don't he trust me?" Mort looked as if his feelings had been hurt.

"It's not that. He wanted everything to look normal. Figured if you didn't know anything was different, you couldn't act different. Ketchum told me over supper last night to bring you up to date first thing this morning."

Just then there was shouting in the street, down the block.

"Fire! Fire! Man the buckets."

Mort Fowler rushed to the door. Jack shouted to halt him.

"Mort, wait. This could be it. A diversion. Give me time to get back in the cell out of sight, then run on out there like you're headed for the fire. Stop as soon as you're safely away from the jail and duck between a couple of buildings where you can still see the door. Then if the McCabes come bustin' in here, you hightail it back."

The deputy waited until Jack had gone into the back, counted to five, then ran out the door. The jailhouse fell silent.

Cash and Avery, on opposite sides of the building, watched as Fowler ran off down the street, then they slipped inside.

"Find the keys," Cash said.

"Here they are." Avery grabbed a ring of keys off a peg by the door to the cell area and they dashed into the back room.

"Oran, we come to get you out!" Cash hollered.

"Cash, Avery—look out! That Dancer kid is here somewhere."

Just then Jack stepped from the open cell at the end of the corridor with his gun drawn.

"Drop 'em, boys. You're covered."

Cash fired a quick shot in Jack's direction, driving him back to shelter, as Avery fumbled with the key to the lock in the door to Oran's cell. Cash dropped to one knee, loosing another shot as Jack peeked from cover.

"Get out. Get out now!" Oran shouted. "It's a trap. Run!"

Avery threw the ring of keys into Oran's cell and dashed through the door to the office. Cash was right behind him.

Sheriff Ketchum's bulky frame blotted out the light of the exit door. The room exploded with the boom of a shotgun and the air clouded instantly with powder smoke. The double blast of buckshot struck Avery McCabe full in the chest, launching him backward into his brother. As their bodies hit the floor, Cash fired at Ketchum, who was hurriedly reloading the ten gauge. The .45 slug from Cash's handgun thudded into the sheriff's right shoulder, spinning him around in the doorway.

Cash scrambled to his feet as Jack Dancer fired from the cell area, coming on the run. McCabe's hat flew from his head as Jack's bullet clipped his ear and he dashed toward the exit, still blocked by the wounded sheriff. At that moment, Deputy Fowler hit the porch at a run and burst through the door, stumbling into Ketchum. Cash fired hurriedly at the floundering deputy and missed. Fowler raised his pistol as Jack came rushing at Cash from behind.

Cash McCabe folded his arms across his face and dove headlong through the window, sending a shower of glass before him. He landed on the back of his neck on the porch, rolled on his shoulders and came up running. As he hit the street, Gunter galloped forward, leading three horses.

Cash sprang into the saddle in a flying mount and the two of them sped down the street while Jack and Fowler got tangled in the doorway. Jack eventually burst into the street, firing after the escaping McCabes. Gunter's horse faltered as a shot struck it, then fell as Gunter jumped into the empty saddle on the back of one of the led horses. They rounded a corner, out of sight.

Jack Dancer pounded down the street after them afoot, his boots raising tiny clouds of dust with every stride.

When Jack walked dejectedly through the door into the sheriff's office, Oran McCabe was on his knees, cradling Avery's still-bleeding corpse in his arms. He had used the key that Avery had pitched through the bars of his cell to open the door, but had not attempted to escape in the confusion that followed, rushing instead to his brother's buckshot-mangled body. He held the dead man to his massive chest, rocking to and fro, crooning like a grieving squaw over a lost child. Jack felt a sudden surge of pity for the hulking killer. After a time, Deputy Fowler pried the body loose from his grasp and led Oran McCabe back to his cell. He offered no resistance and seemed oblivious to anyone or anything outside his grief.

"Let hisself out with the key," Mort said, looking puzzled. "Didn't even try to get away. Just fell on this body and started wallerin'."

As the doctor worked over Sheriff Ketchum's wound, Jack reported that the remaining McCabe boys had made clean their escape.

"I'll stay 'til Oran's safely hung," Jack told the lawman, "then I'll be going after them."

"Can't I persuade you to stay on a while, Dancer? Least 'til this shoulder heals?"

Jack shook his head. "Sorry, Sheriff. Can't afford to fall too far behind them. Mort's a good man. He can run things, with your counsel to guide him."

The next morning found Jack Dancer sitting with his legs dangling off the edge of the porch that fronted the jailhouse. He watched grimly as they led Oran McCabe from his cell and toward the gallows. The condemned man had again assumed his surly attitude and swaggering manner. As Mort Fowler steered him through the packed street, McCabe glowered at the gathered spectators. Men and women alike shrank from the menace in his glaring eyes.

Jack felt a presence behind him. When he turned around to look, his Colt .44 was in his hand.

"Howdy, Jack."

"John!" He smiled broadly at the unexpected sight of his uncle. "What are you doing here? I mean, how—"

"You're not the only Dancer can read a paper, boy. I come to see McCabe get his due."

John plopped down beside his nephew and pointed to the scaffold, drawing Jack's attention back to the proceedings. McCabe stood behind the dangling noose as Deputy Fowler bound his ankles. The local parson was reading a passage from the Bible, but the words were swallowed up by the anticipatory mumblings of the onlookers. The preacher then asked Oran if he had anything he wished to say before he met his Maker. A hush fell over the crowd.

"Yeah, I got somethin' to say, psalm-singer. Go kiss your sister." He looked out upon the upturned faces of the spectators. "That goes for all of you. I'll meet every one of you in bloody hell!"

McCabe spit into the audience, scattering folks and clearing a wide circle directly in front of the gallows. The hangman stepped forward and offered him a black hood. Oran defiantly shook him off. Then the noose was dropped over his head. The executioner snugged the hemp tight behind the left ear. At a signal from the judge on the platform, a lever was pulled and the floor opened beneath the big man's feet. The crack of Oran McCabe's neck breaking was clearly audible in the clear mountain air, and an awed moaning rippled through the gathering.

It had been early in the morning when the attempted jailbreak had taken place, but this was a frontier community and its people were early risers.

Jack and John each canvassed a section of homes and businesses along the McCabes' escape route from Fort Collins, asking every resident, owner, and clerk if they had seen the fleeing men. The commotion caused by the fire at the livery and the deadly reports of gunfire at the jail had brought many of them to their doors, windows, and stoops to investigate. The eyewitness reports the Dancers gathered allowed them to trace the progress of the fugitives' flight away from the little town. The McCabes had headed north, taking a trail that led toward Cheyenne, in Wyoming Territory. Jack and John Dancer bought supplies, packed their gear, and mounted their pursuit.

It was the spring of 1883. Chester A. Arthur, who had become President in '81 after Garfield was assassinated, was in the White House in Washington City. He was currently being criticized for his three-hour lunch breaks and four-day work week.

In the big eastern cities, Thomas Edison's electric lamps were being used to light commercial buildings. There was even talk of playing a night baseball game under electric lights this year in Fort Wayne, Indiana.

Faust was playing at the new Metropolitan Opera House in New York City, and a bunch of pushy ladies had formed something called the Women's Temperance Union, vowing to put an end to the selling and drinking of whiskey.

Closer to home, W. F. "Buffalo Bill" Cody was putting together a Wild West Show, and a renegade Apache war chief named Geronimo was raising a ruckus down in Arizona and New Mexico Territories.

Astounding cultural and technical advancements were rapidly transforming the face of the populated East, but in most areas west of the Mississippi, the force of law was a sometimes thing. The western frontier remained rowdy, ribald and hard to curry. It was a wide, wild country that tested the mettle of all who roamed its trackless reaches, where a man did what he had to do.

"Whoa up a minute here, Jack."

John alighted from the black and dropped to one knee, studying tracks in the mud where a seep crossed the trail. He nodded his head and swung back into the saddle.

"Same tracks as outside Fort Collins," he told his partner as they rode. "We're still a ways behind. I figure they'll stop in Cheyenne. We'll ride on, try to pick up the trail again there."

John Dancer had spent a good portion of his life away from the restraints and structures of towns and cities. He was a man who loved untamed, unpeopled lands and he knew the wilderness like the back of his hand. Years spent chasing wild horses over the vast, windblown expanses of the high plains had sharpened his skills of tracking and observation, and he could read a trail as well as any man, red or white. He had stayed among the Indians, had traded with them, hunted with them, called many of them friend. And from them he had learned to track a man or a beast by the trail left by the mind of his quarry as well as from the prints left on the ground by its passing. He could identify the hoofprints of a particular horse as certainly as most men would attach an identity to a man's signature on a sheet of paper. As they rode together, Jack began to learn these things too.

He also learned that it was not as easy for a man to lose himself in the lonely, untraveled wilderness as one might think, for a man on the run must have water, food, and shelter. A good hunter could generally stay close to his prey by searching out these sources of supply.

The McCabes, they knew, were not experienced frontiersmen. They had spent their lives in the plush surroundings of civilization that their father's money had afforded them. They were tough men, true, but they were dependent upon the services rendered by other people for their survival. They would most likely stick to traveled trails where stores and outposts were handy for supplying their daily needs. That would make the chase simpler. The Dancers need only stay on their trail and keep the pressure on.

"Think they know they're being followed?" Jack asked.

"I figure they do."

"Then we'd best expect trouble."

"You got always to expect it," John said. "When you start hunting men, be mindful that they can hunt as well. Always pays to stay on your toes. This is rough country, with plenty of places for a man to lie in wait. Keep your mind lookin' around every bend and behind every rock."

"You figure they'll keep moving, then?" Jack said.

"Wouldn't you?"

And that was the start of it, the beginning of many long weeks of relentless pursuit, weeks in which Jack and John Dancer kept doggedly to the trail of the men they sought during every waking moment. Weeks in which they gave the McCabes no rest, no time to gather their forces, to spend their money, to enjoy the healing comfort of saloons or the sweet companionship of the fairer sex.

The chase took them across the lower reaches of the Wyoming Territory, down into Utah Territory and finally back into Colorado.

The Dancers found evidence of the brothers' passing in towns, mining camps, at ranches and homesteads, at trading posts—places the McCabes had stopped for supplies or to eat or to rest, and at each of the locations they inquired after the outlaws, the story of the manhunt was left behind. Soon Jack and John began to discover that folks knew who they were, and of their mission. The West was a big place, sparsely populated, but many of its people were movers and nomads, and news had a way of getting there ahead of a man. Folks liked a good yarn, and the story of the Dancers and the McCabes made good campfire chatter.

There was not a cowboy in the West that did not know the names of the best of the gunfighters, know what they had done and where they were at any given time. Reputations were begun in the dusty streets of frontier towns and across the blazing barrels of six-guns, but they were made and spread around campfires and in the saloons. It was, indeed, a big country, but an extremely hard place to keep a secret.

Harried and worn, Cash McCabe pulled the saddle from his horse and dropped it to the ground. He kicked a pine cone, sending it bouncing across the clearing. He pulled off his hat and slapped it testily against his leg.

"I've had enough of this foolishness, Gunter."

The albino pulled long on the canteen he had tipped to his lips, wiped his mouth on his sleeve, capped it and looked at Cash.

"What foolishness?"

"Running. Hiding. I need to smell me some perfume on a lady, 'stead of smelling you stinking up the air around me like a warthog. 'Stead of smelling myself and thinking it's my horse. I need to eat somebody else's cooking and drink me a washtub full of whiskey. Need to hear folks laughing. I'm sick of looking over my dadgum shoulder, Gunter, and I'm sick of you."

"Well, shoot, it ain't my fault," Gunter said, puffing up like a horned toad.

"Never said it was. But riding with you is like blowing a cavalry bugle to let those Dancers know where we're at. In case you haven't noticed, brother, you stick out in a crowd. You might as well be blue or green."

"What in tarnation you expect me to do about it, pig-brain? Lay out in the sun 'til I burn black?"

"No. I don't care what you do. I'm taking off on my own. They can't follow both of us at once, unless they split up too. And I can handle either one of them by hisself."

"Cash . . . you serious? You and me are all the family we got left. We'd ought to stick together."

"We can meet up somewheres later, after we lose those Dancers, or kill them."

Gunter slipped off the side of his horse and rushed to face his brother.

"That's it, Cash. We can lay for 'em. Wait for them to catch up to us and kill them. What do you say?"

Cash looked at the pleading, paste-white face of his brother. He was sick of the sight of him, sick of the sound of his voice. But darn it, he was right. They were family.

"Alright, Gunter, alright. We'll do it your way." He pulled his .45 and held it in front of his face. His gray eyes were as cold as the steel of the shiny barrel in which they were reflected. "We'll kill them."

Chapter Sixteen

The Dancers stopped to make camp on Whitewater Creek, north of the Gunnison near Grand Mesa. Great cliffs and mounds of red and yellow rock were crested with fire as the sun made an unhurried trek toward the windswept plateaus to the west, filling gulches and arroyos with blackness in the wake of its retreat.

They had a light supper of cold beans and jerky, washed it down with a pot of coffee, then turned to their blankets. Jack was still worrying over the spot he had selected to lay his bed, clearing it of rocks and sticks, when he heard the heavy, even breathing of deep sleep coming from his uncle's direction. He envied the older man his ability to fall immediately into a restful sleep. John's years of living under an open sky had taught him that a man had best rest, eat, and drink when the opportunity was present, for one never knew when the chance might come again.

Jack stretched out and pulled the blanket to his chin, scooting his body this way and that until he got comfortable. He folded his hands behind his head and stared up at the slowly emerging stars winking through a ragged covering of wispy purple clouds. He raised himself on one

elbow, dug under the ground cover beneath him and extracted a small stone. He tossed it aside and settled down
again, wondering why, no matter how carefully you swept
the ground beneath your bed, there was always one more
rock to devil a man.

He thought about the chase in which he and John per-
sisted, wondering when and how it would end. Were they
doing the right thing? He was not sure anymore. His hatred
had cooled and hardened into steely resolve. What lay between the Dancers and the McCabes was a simple matter
of justice. They traveled in a land where no law existed
beyond the borders of towns and it fell to each man to right
the wrongs done to him and to those under his care. Should
Cash and Gunter be allowed to roam free, they would
surely continue to ravage the innocent, as they had done to
Tom and Grace Dancer.

And what did he, himself, have in his future? He had an
offer from Sam Coffee to wear a badge, but Jack did not
want to live his life with his fist wrapped around the butt
of a six-gun. He darn sure would not go back to farming,
and working cattle was not what he wanted. He thought
perhaps he would like to have a spread someplace where
he could raise horses, maybe partner with John. He realized, though, that for now he had best keep his mind geared
to the task at hand, to the pursuit of the McCabes, or he
might not be alive to fret over things yet to come.

Would he ever see Laura again? It had been in his mind,
back there in Ouray, to spend the rest of his days with her
beside him. To raise a family of strong sons to carry on
the Dancer name. The memory of holding her in his arms
excited him, and for a moment he could almost feel the
softness of her hand as it caressed his cheek. He quickly
pushed the thought from his mind. Laura was gone, running
away from a past that was not even her own. Where was
she? Was she alright? Would she find someone else? His

eyes popped open at that thought and he felt a ball of fear form in his chest. He tossed around in his blankets.

"You better get some rest, boy. Daylight's right around the corner, and we've hard riding to do," John said softly from his bedroll.

Jack settled back and closed his eyes. He heard the call of a coyote from the far reaches of the mesa, a lonely cry that only served to deepen his melancholy.

Gunter scrambled down from the rocky vista where he had been perched the better part of the day. He made his way down the talus slope toward camp, half running, half sliding. Cash was sitting at the edge of a small fire, feeding sticks to the hungry blaze for want of something better to do.

"They're coming," Gunter shouted excitedly, "they're coming."

Cash jumped up. "Well shut your big mouth, they might hear you."

Gunter shook his head. He held out a mariner's glass.

"No they won't. Too far out yet. Probably two and a half, three miles. But it's them. I recognized that buckskin Jack Dancer rides."

Cash scattered the fire with his foot, then bent down and scooped up a double fistful of dirt and sprinkled it over the coals.

"Okay. It's almost dark. Timing couldn't be better. You get back up in that nest of rocks you were in. You'll have a clear shot from there. I'll find me a spot over across the trail. We'll get them from both directions.

"Take John Dancer first. He's the dangerous one. Besides, that stinkin' kid is mine. I got a bullet with his name on it. Now get to it. It's time this was ended."

Gunter turned and hurried back toward his lookout in the

boulders on the west side of the trail. Cash grabbed his Winchester out of the saddle scabbard at his feet, started away, then halted. He leaned the gun against a tree and began to saddle the horses and break camp. When he was done, he reclaimed the rifle and scurried across the trail into a thick stand of alder.

The moon was on the rise as the Dancers approached.

"You 'bout ready to call it a day, partner?" Jack asked.

"I reckon," John said. "Let's get over that rise yonder. Looks like there's good cover there."

"How far behind are we, John?"

"Tracks I seen before sundown looked to be about a day old, or less. If they haven't stopped somewhere, we can catch them in a day and a half, riding hard. But keep alert. They could be holed up anywhere."

"I've had a funny feeling the last day or so that this hunt is about over," Jack said. "Can't happen soon enough for me."

Suddenly John halted his horse. He had seen the moon reflect off something in the rocks ahead of them, a reflection that did not belong in the wilderness. Jack was riding a few feet ahead. John spurred the black and left his saddle in a flying dive, driving a hard shoulder into Jack's back and sending them both plummeting to the rocky ground as the ugly whine of a bullet pierced the air. The sound of a rifle shot sounded a split second later, fouling the silence of the night with a resounding boom and sending the horses screaming back down the trail at a full run. Both men scrambled for cover.

Jack was pounding furiously toward a gully off to the right when he realized that John was not behind him. He came to a skidding halt and wheeled around. John was on his belly, crawling after him. He was hit! Jack dropped to his hands and knees and skittered like a crab to his uncle. He grabbed him under the arms and pulled him toward the dropoff while bullets pocked the ground around them, sending up geysers of dirt and rock. They slid over the rim into the shallow gully, hugging the bank and clawing at their belts for their guns.

"How bad you hit?"

"Don't rightly know. Got me in the hip, feels like. I'll worry about it later."

"John," Jack said, "thanks. You saved my bacon."

"Naw," he said, "I was diving for cover and you got in my way."

Jack smiled. "Where'd the shots come from?"

They peeked over the lip of the dry wash in which they lay and John indicated a high pinnacle of rocks ahead of them and to the left.

"Up there, about ten feet down from the top."

"I'm going after him," Jack said, pushing himself erect with his palms against the slope of the draw. "Then we'll get you to a doctor."

"Don't hurry on my account, boy. Keep to the bed of this ditch as far as you can, and don't stop in one spot no longer than you have to. Keep moving, keep low and keep your eyes open. Remember, there are two of them."

But there were not to be two of them for long. At the first rifle report, Cash had made his way to the edge of the trees and looked out at the Dancers disappearing into the gully, both still alive, both armed and able to fight. He quickly worked his way down the slope to the camp where he had left the horses tethered. Giving a last look to the rocky redoubt where his brother lay firing down on their pursuers, he stepped into the dun's leather and, leading the pack horse, rode off into the night, away from the scene of the gun battle that was sure to follow.

"Sorry, brother," he said in an inaudible whisper, "I hope you come out on top in this deal, but if only one of us is to live to carry on the proud name of McCabe, it had best be me. It wouldn't do to have a whole raft of pink-eyed, bleached-out descendants."

Meanwhile, Jack was creeping cautiously along the base of the tower of rocks from which the rifleman had loosed his sniping attack. Though the night was cool, his brow was beaded with sweat. He would have preferred meeting his attacker face to face. It was a scary thing to advance toward a man that wanted you dead, not knowing exactly where he was. He dried the sweaty palm of his gun hand on the leg of his britches and glanced back toward the spot where John was hidden. In the moon's meager light, he could barely make out the black gash of the depression. He was worried. John's pants had been soaked black with lost blood. He needed a doctor soon, and it was a long ride to any help that Jack knew of. Telluride was the closest town of any size. A sense of urgency gripped him as he turned his attention back to the towering jumble of boulders.

Jack snaked through the brush at the base of the rock pylon, searching for a way to the top. He ducked his head suddenly as a shadowy form darted across his line of vision. A bat. He took a deep breath to put his heart back where it belonged.

There—an opening in the rock pile. He ducked through, pausing to allow his eyes to adjust to the darker shadows. He saw a ladder-like trail of depressions leading upward into the heart of the rock tower. He holstered his gun to free his hands, then cautiously and quietly started to climb. His boots made small, crunching noises on the loose pebbles that covered the irregular steps of the ascending path.

Jack topped out in a small, bowl-shaped nest that overlooked the trail below. This was the spot where the sniper had been hidden, alright, but there was no one here now. A glint caught the corner of his eye and he bent to pick a shell casing off the ground at his feet. A glance around located several more spent cartridges. Where had the rifleman gone, and why had he abandoned his position? Was he down there now, advancing on the gully where John lay wounded and bleeding? Jack started back down, stepping carefully to avoid slipping on the treacherous footing of the rock ladder. He reached the bottom and slid back out into the open, turning his attention toward the gully. As his head came around, he was looking into a black hole as big as a washtub—the end of a rifle barrel.

"Got you, Dancer."

The albino grinned from behind the sights of the rifle, enjoying the startled and helpless look on his captive's face. The man's white skin appeared translucent and spectral in the faint light cast by the early moon, and the pupils of his eyes showed red, like the eyes of a hungry wolf reflecting a campfire's glow. The taste of fear was bitter in Jack Dancer's mouth as he looked upon the face of death.

"Throw your weapon over here by me," Gunter said, "real easy like."

Jack unleathered his .44 and tossed it on the ground at Gunter McCabe's feet.

"Now, where's the other one? Where is John Dancer?"

"I'll call him out," Jack said, stalling for time.

He had an idea. A slim chance, but one he knew he must take. It was nighttime, so Gunter McCabe was not wearing his dark-lensed spectacles. Jack turned slightly away and slid his fingers into his vest pocket, palming a match. Then he put his arm up as if to lean against the rock.

He struck the match against the rough surface of the boulder and thrust it toward Gunter's face. The albino recoiled from the glare of the flame like a vampire shrinking from a silver cross. Jack swatted the rifle aside as Gunter stumbled backward, weak eyes watering, blinded by the flash of the match.

Jack drove a shoulder hard into the other man's gut, sending the rifle skidding across the rocky ground and into the brush. Gunter wrested free. Both men scrambled for Jack's discarded Colt, which lay on the ground between them. Gunter slapped a white hand around the butt of the .44 and his finger slipped into the trigger guard. Jack grabbed the barrel, trying to wrench the weapon free. The two enemies grappled face to face, chest to chest. Suddenly the gun bucked between them and the deafening blast of a shot halted the struggle.

Gunter took a stumbling step backward as he got to his feet. He stared at Jack with a look of confusion and disbelief in his pink eyes, then looked to watch the blood that oozed between his fingers where he clutched at the hole in his gut. He noted with a small measure of satisfaction that his blood, at least, was as red as any man's.

The pale gunman wished now that he had led a better life, but no man had ever explained it to him quite this way before.

"You're dying, McCabe," Jack said. "Where's your brother?"

Gunter thought that was a reasonable question. He felt the strength leaving his legs and allowed himself to wilt slowly to the ground, landing in a sitting position.

"Go to blazes" were Gunter McCabe's final words.

In searching the area for Cash McCabe, Jack discovered the tracks left by the departing horses and recognized the now-familiar print of Cash's lineback dun. He hurried back to the gully where he had left John.

John Dancer was lying on his side, weak but awake. Enlisting him to hold a lighted match, Jack examined the bloody injury low on his uncle's side. It was deep and ragged, but the ricocheting bullet had not hit the hip bone, and the bleeding seemed to have stopped. Jack stuffed his neckerchief into the wound, then gathered wood for a fire. When the blaze was well started, he hurried down the sloping trail to retrieve their horses. When he got back with the still-skittish animals, John was unconscious.

At that high altitude the air was thin and pure, so infection was not a big worry if one kept the injured area clean. Jack heated water over the fire, bathed and bandaged John's raw wound as best he could, then brewed up a broth of shaved jerky, flour, and water. When John woke up, Jack gave him a drink of water, then spooned the soup down him.

After he had done what he could for his ailing trailmate and had him bedded down for the night, Jack dragged Gunter's body to the gully. They had no shovel with which to bury the dead outlaw, so he caved a bank in on top of the body, then piled a few rocks on top of the mound for good measure. The crude interment would not prevent the scavengers of the wild from discovering the corpse, but it would delay their grisly feast for awhile yet.

The next morning, Jack stripped Gunter McCabe's saddle horse of its trappings and turned it loose. Some fortunate roving Indian would most likely find the animal and decide that the Great Spirit wanted him to have it as a gift. Then Jack tied John in the saddle on the big black and they headed at an easy pace for Telluride.

"The doctor says you'll mend good as new, John. You probably won't be laid up more than two or three weeks. You are in good hands here," Jack said. "I'll be riding out after Cash McCabe in the morning."

John pushed himself up off the pillow, resting on his elbows.

"You figgerin' to go without me?"

Jack nodded. "You're the one said we need to keep the pressure on. I can't let up on him now. I got it to do."

"How do you expect to find him? You can't track worth a darn."

"Not so, friend," Jack said, grinning. "I been riding with John Dancer. He's a man can track a fish through muddy water, a dung beetle in a sandstorm, or a bird through the night sky. Told me so himself. I'm bound to have learned some. Learned to be too stinkin' rock-headed to give up on a thing, if nothing else."

John plopped back onto the bed, looking disgusted.

"Alright, dadgum it, have it your way. But if you wander off and get yourself killed, don't come cryin' to me."

So he stocked his saddlebags with Arbuckle's coffee and .44 cartridges, pointed his buckskin's nose for the high ridges, and, with the rising sun at his back, Jack Dancer took to the trail once more in his relentless pursuit of Cash McCabe.

Chapter Seventeen

It started to rain—a cold drizzle that drew a curtain of gunmetal gray across the fading evening. The boughs of the trees were a richer, deeper green under the influence of the pewter clouds that obscured the crowns of the towering evergreens, and their great trunks rose like columns of iron in the mist.

Jack had been eight days on the trail without word or a sign of the man he was seeking. He had started his search at the scene of the battle with Gunter McCabe, following the direction of the path Cash had taken from the camp, though the tracks no longer existed. He was now in a primitive area of the high San Juans, riding the Continental Divide near Wolf Creek Pass. He was cold, tired and wet, and almost out of supplies. He had begun to survey the forest around him for a place to hole up for the night when he spotted a thin tendril of smoke climbing lazily from the vale below him. He turned the buckskin down the slope.

A long, low building made of logs was set back in a sheltering grove of juniper. It looked to be an old trading post, and it had surely seen better days, but it beckoned to Jack like a fine hotel in Denver. He walked his horse to the yard and dismounted, ground-tying the tired animal with a long lead to allow it freedom to graze on the sweet grasses at the edge of the trees.

Jack walked to the door of the post and entered, bending over to avoid the low beam that topped the opening. Once in, he was forced to pause to allow his eyes to adjust to the dim, dingy light. The air inside was heavy with the foul odors of uncured hides, unwashed bodies, and raw whiskey. Jack shucked his slicker and walked into the room.

A woman in men's clothing stood behind a bar contrived of a couple of long, rough planks laid atop empty whiskey barrels. She was a burly woman with thick arms, huge pendulous breasts that sagged to her waist, and a figure that looked like boiled-over grits fleeing a pot. Her hair was matted and tangled, and hung over her forehead into piggy little eyes. She smiled as she saw the stranger enter, exposing a grin that boasted only three brown teeth.

"Come in here, honey, out of that rotten weather. How's about a glass of whiskey to cut the chill?"

She produced a cloudy bottle of liquor that Jack guessed was mostly Piedra River and chewing tobacco. He declined the drink, handing her a list of supplies.

"Just fill this list, please, ma'am . . . Been a man through here lately?" Jack asked, "Big man on a lineback dun? Name's McCabe, though I doubt he'd give it."

A hushed mumbling behind him spun Jack around. Two filthy men wrapped in shaggy skin coats were lounging on a pile of hides in a dark corner, sharing a bottle. They stared at the newcomer like he was a piece of fresh meat. Jack felt a queasiness in the pit of his stomach, a feeling that something was amiss. He reached to his hip and flipped the rawhide thong off the cocking piece of his Colt.

"Git him," one of the men yelled as they pulled their pistols in unison. Jack dove for a post as both men fired. His .44 spoke and one of the hiders went down. Jack flipped a round-top table over on its edge and ducked behind it as the second man fired again.

A shuffling behind him whipped his head around to see the woman lunging toward him, an ax poised above her head. Jack rolled aside to avoid her murderous fury as the man behind him fired once more, missing Jack and placing a neat, purple hole in the center of the charging woman's forehead. She dropped like a felled ox.

Jack shot again. The man flew off his feet, landing heavily on the pile of smelly hides. Blood gushed from a hole at the base of his throat, drenching the wolfskin coat he wore. Jack grabbed the table and pulled himself to his feet, breathing heavily.

Both the woman and the man who took Jack's last bullet were dead. The other hider was bleeding profusely from a wound in his thigh. Jack crossed to him and placed the barrel of his pistol under the whimpering man's nose.

"Why'd you jump me, you smelly coyote? Why?"

"I'm shot. Oh, lord, I'm shot."

He ceased whining at the sound of the cocking of the gun under his nose, withering beneath the stern gaze of the man he had tried to murder.

"That feller you was askin' after," the hider said, "he come through and give us fifty dollars, sayin' if you come along, we was to kill you."

"How was he to know you wouldn't just take his money and do nothing?" Jack asked him.

"He was going to give us another hunnerd if we brung him your head in a toesack."

Jack backed away and holstered his gun, shaken by what he had just learned. It had never occurred to him that McCabe would try to *hire* him killed. He knew the McCabe brothers had crossed the line from ruffians and bullies to vicious outlaws some time back, but somehow he had figured them to be men who would do their own killing. The attempt on his life by Blackjack Daniels in Tascosa had been the doing of old Dad McCabe. Now it appeared that Cash was of the same bent. He would need to watch his backtrail from here on out, and trust no one he met along the way.

"Where were you to meet McCabe to collect your money?" Jack asked the cowering hider.

"Down around Durango, south and west of here. An old abandoned silver mine down there, The Lady Beth. Said he'd meet us there."

Jack walked behind the bar and began to gather the supplies he needed from stock on shelves along the wall. He tied the burlap bag and strode purposefully across the dirt floor toward the entrance. The wounded man called after him.

"Hey, Mister, you ain't goin' to just leave me here? I need a doctor!"

"If I run across one that shows an interest in your case, I'll tell him where to find you."

He closed the door behind him as he left.

The Lady Beth Silver Mine was a black hole carved into the almost perpendicular face of an unnamed peak towering above the rushing rapids of the Los Piños River. The abandoned diggings were accessible only by way of a narrow zigzag trail that had been laboriously chiseled into the rocky face of the steep incline, starting at the river's edge and meandering back and forth along the precipitous slope to the mine entrance several hundred feet above.

Jack Dancer sat his saddle, his head craned back, surveying the situation. He did not like it a bit. A man caught on the face of that mountain would be an easy target for a rifleman from either the foot of the trail below or the mouth of the Lady Beth above. No sir, Jack did not like this deal at all. Still, he had come after Cash McCabe, and if the outlaw was in that mine, that is where Jack would go.

He tethered his horse and unlimbered his Henry from the saddle scabbard, then walked to the base of the trail. He knelt down to examine the rocky surface of the path. The thick layer of dust had been disturbed, indicating recent use, but there had been no activity that day, nor probably the day before. The scuffed marks of passage were covered with a thin, even coat of dust. If McCabe was in the mine shaft, he had been there a while. Maybe he had come and gone. One way to find out. Jack started climbing.

At each switchback in the trail he paused to check both above and below, fully expecting an attack at any moment, but no rifleman appeared to pick him off the mountainside and he topped out on a wide ledge at the mine entrance. He leaned his rifle against a rock and drew his handgun.

"McCabe! This is Jack Dancer. Come out. Come out and face me."

His only answer was the echo of his own voice from the depths of the mine. Quickly, he slipped inside, flattening himself against the rock wall at the mouth of the tunnel.

Deciding that he must be alone, Jack located a lantern. He sloshed it back and forth. Half full of fuel, by the heft and sound of it. He lit the wick, held the lantern aloft, above the brim of his hat, and advanced into the mine.

Further along the shaft he found a spot where someone had camped. Had spent several days here by the looks of the scattered debris. Cigarette butts, a whiskey bottle, several empty tins. The remains of a fire. Had it been Cash McCabe?

Jack was suddenly seized by a flash of anger and frustration. He kicked at the sooty remains of the cookfire.

"Blast it," he said aloud, "another dead end . . . *dead end . . . end . . . end.*" The echo of his words mocked his fury.

Jack made a rapid descent down the trail to the river. He

had wasted most of a day checking out the Lady Beth, and he was hopeful of making Durango by nightfall. It would help his disposition to sleep in a real bed and to eat a hot meal prepared by someone else's hand.

When he reached his horse he found a man hunched over a hat-sized fire, brewing a pot of coffee. Jack recognized the pot as his own.

"Howdy, hoss," the stranger said. "Coffee's purt'nigh ready. Borrowed the fixin's from your possibles. Hope you don't mind."

He was an old gaffer. A weathered, lean strip of hide in a battered bowler hat and ragged clothes that had never known the luxury of laundering. He wore a scruffy, mul-ticolored beard that put Jack in mind of the hide of a brindle steer, and his drooping mustaches showed the effects of repeated exposure to eruptions of streams of tobacco juice. Lively eyes sparkled like new pennies set in the craggy, sun-browned features of his thin face.

"You'd be Jack Dancer," the old man stated positively.

"That takes care of me. Who the blazes are you?"

He cackled. "Been called most ever'thing, but most folks hereabouts know me as Packrat Pete."

"How do you know me?" Jack asked, accepting a cup of coffee from Pete's gnarled fist.

"The other feller, he told me you'd be comin'."

"McCabe?"

"That's what he called hisself. Said to tell you he ain't runnin' no more. Sick of it, he said. Told me to let you know he'd be waitin' for you at Mesa Verde, day after tomorrow. Said you should come shootin'."

"How do I know you're telling the truth? He might have paid you to throw me off his trail."

The old man's features clouded. He swigged down the cupful of scalding coffee in a single gulp.

"Makes me no never mind, sonny, where you go or what

you do. I've made and lost four fortunes in my lifetime, and money ain't never been a thing I treasured over my word. Thanks for the coffee."

The old denizen of the desert got to his feet and started toward a burro that was tied next to Jack's horse.

"Mister Packrat, sir," Jack called out, "wait. I apologize. This hunt has got me distrustful of everyone I come across. McCabe has paid money to have me killed. Reckon I've gotten jumpy."

Packrat Pete hopped onto the back of his donkey with a quick and sprightly move. He turned to Jack.

"Don't fret on it, sonny. I understand, and I got me no way of knowing if that other feller was tellin' it to me straight or not. I was just passin' it along.

"He looks to be a mean one, Dancer," Packrat Pete said. "I figger he don't have the scruples of a wild dog.

"So you ride careful, hear? Mesa Verde is full of old cliff dwellings, with a thousand places for a man to hide. It was the home of the Ancient Ones . . . a haunted place. I'd steer clear of there, was I you. Wait him out."

With that the old man threw his hand into the air in a farewell salute and jabbed his heels into the little burro's sides, starting away. Jack watched him from sight, then turned his eyes to the southwest, toward Mesa Verde.

Jack reined the buckskin into a stand of juniper and dismounted. He pulled the bandana from around his neck, removed his hat and wiped the sweat and grit off his forehead, then ran the neckerchief around the inside band of his Stetson. He lifted the canteen from the saddle, took a long pull, then poured water into the hat and held it to the horse's muzzle.

He slapped the dripping hat back on his head, walked to the edge of the trees and peered out over the vast windswept expanse of sage, checking his backtrail. As he watched, a pair of dust devils formed and began to glide spectrally across the naked plain, like diaphanous spirits performing a mating dance. He stepped back into the saddle and urged the big horse out of the trees.

Broad, flat-topped mesas rose before him like battlements against the turquoise sky, standing rooted and indestructible in sunlight and silence. The Mesa Verde. He was riding upon a great tableland, a fantastic realm of rock slashed by immense canyons and gashed by gulches, washes, and arroyos. Jack nosed his horse down a slope and into a narrow canyon, seeking to escape the exposed position he had been holding on the rim.

He rounded the base of a jagged tower of rock. Suddenly, unexpectedly, there it was: an ancient cliff dwelling set in the sheer face of the opposite wall of the canyon; a miniature terraced city of soft pink stone, safely isolated in a high cranny of the dark, shaggy cliffs; an island, fragile but indestructible, aloof from the flow of moving time. Jack spurred the buckskin into a trot.

Piñon and juniper grew along the base of the cliff and Jack could see several small springs feeding into placid pools on the canyon floor. He stopped at one of these pools to refill his canteen and to allow his horse to drink its fill. He stood back from the wall, looking up, wondering how the Ancient Ones had gotten down to the water and up again. He spotted what looked to have been a ladder. The wood was remarkably preserved and solid, but whatever had held the rungs in place had rotted away centuries before. He would have to find another entry.

He had no idea just where in this rugged mesa country he might find trace of Cash McCabe. He would search the cliff dwellings first, then if he found no sign of the man, he would cast about for tracks. He looked up again at the cavity in the wall of the mesa. Perhaps there was a way down from the top.

Jack rode the floor of the canyon until he spotted a game trail leading upward, then urged his mount onto the narrow path to the top of the mesa, emerging on a tree-covered tableland. He trotted back to a spot on the rim above the cliff city, swung down from the saddle and tied the horse in the trees out of sight. He noticed a faint trail leading down to the cave, so, taking up his canteen and saddlebags, he followed it. It turned into a narrow rock ledge that ran for a hundred yards or so along the face of the cliff toward the dwellings. He reached a spot where, centuries past, a cleft in the rock had been walled up. A narrow tunnel was fashioned in the base of the wall. He dropped to his hands and knees to peer into the dark opening. He could see light on the other side. Jack hesitated. He did not like tight places. He had an uneasy premonition that something evil lurked beyond the wall, and he remembered the old man's warning that these cliff houses were haunted by the ancient dead. He grinned at the fear he was feeling as he started to crawl.

When Jack emerged from the tunnel he was in a mammoth cave more than three hundred feet wide and ninety feet deep. The houses of the village were piled one atop the other at the back of the depression, the top of the cave overhanging the stone structures to form a protective roof. The front of the cave was one big courtyard with a low, crumbling parapet built along the cliff edge.

The structures themselves were of smooth-hewn sandstone blocks held together by clay masonry. Small stones had been embedded in the clay for added strength. The roofs were made of wooden beams and branches, plastered over with clay. Some of the dwellings had low, narrow doors, barely big enough to accommodate Jack's wide shoulders. Many had no door at all, only an opening in the roof, and Jack found evidence of ladders used to enter these rooms. The walls of the building were plumb, except for a few towers that were perfectly round. Narrow walks and balconies extended outside the houses under the doorways of the upper stories, leading from one room to the next.

Jack began to go through the dwellings one by one, his .44 in his fist, searching for Cash McCabe. There was no reason for him to think that the man he was chasing was in these ruins. He was probably up top somewhere, or crawling around in one of the many canyons of the mesa. But Jack had learned that in the wilds, the less than cautious wind up dead, so he would be ready.

He completed his tour of the cliff dwelling, finding a variety of things left behind by the Ancient Ones that indicated they had been hunters and farmers—stone knives, arrowheads and other implements, a primitive wooden digging stick or hoe, the bones of turkeys, deer, and mountain sheep. Jack also found tiny dried ears of corn, bean and squash seeds, and the husks of piñon nuts.

Most of the rooms had niches in them for storage and decaying wooden pegs set in the walls, on which to hang things. Each room measured about eight feet by six feet, and the walls were plastered with clay and decorated with geometric designs and crude figures of birds and small animals. A few of the walls had crumbled and filled the rooms with rubble.

Jack found several round underground chambers, kivas, each with walls about six feet high, floors of packed earth, and a shallow fire pit before an L-shaped shaft. Each kiva had six masonry pillars that supported a roof fashioned of logs and covered with a layer of soil.

In one of the stone cubicles, Jack kicked at a mound of dirt and unearthed a cloth-wrapped human skeleton. A skull rolled toward his feet, its toothy mouth frozen in an eternal smile, and Jack skittered through the door into the courtyard. *That was enough exploring for one day.*

The opposite wall of the canyon was turning lilac in the

dusk. Jack decided to spend the night in the cave, not wanting to crawl back through that tunnel and climb the narrow ledge in the dim light. He rounded up some sticks and built a fire in a pit that had been hollowed out in the cave floor outside the dwellings. Then he fetched his saddlebags and canteen to start a pot of coffee.

A faint, faraway moaning sound wafted through the cave. Jack jerked his head around. Was it the wind through the openings of the cliff houses? The wail of a wolf from the mesa top? Or—

Jack Dancer pushed the notion of spirits and haunts from his mind and settled back to watch the coffee boil.

Chapter Eighteen

Dawn announced its coming with a shattering clap of thunder that brought Jack awake with his Colt in his hand. He looked around to orient himself, rubbed a callused palm across his face, and self-consciously slipped the gun back into its leather nest.

"Getting a little jumpy, there, Dancer," he said aloud, admonishing himself.

He unfolded, hopped to his feet, stepped under his hat, and went to rekindle the fire from the night before. He used the last of the water from his canteen to start a pot of coffee, sat by the fire and began cleaning his revolver. Looking out across the canyon, he saw that it had started to storm, and an aggressive wind was pushing the rain down the canyon in silver sheets. The overhang of the cave protected him from the downpour, but he thought of his horse, still tethered in the trees atop the mesa, and he began to gather his things. He reached for the coffeepot at the fire's edge.

The tin pot was snatched violently from his hand as the sound of a shot rang out in the cave, echoing off the ancient walls of the pueblo. The coffeepot flew over the cliff's edge, clanking against the rock face to the canyon floor below.

Jack scrambled to his feet and made a weaving dash for the dwellings as more bullets nipped at his heels and pocked the cave floor around him. He had been cleaning his gun, so the cylinder was empty of shells. He filled his fist with ammunition from his belt as he ran, trying awkwardly to reload as he made for the safety of the cliff houses. He made a headlong dive through a narrow doorway, scraping his shoulder and landing in a heap inside a room.

The roof of the stone cubicle in which he had taken refuge was timeworn and full of gaps and holes, offering him a patchy view of the terraced houses above. He glimpsed a fleeting shadow disappearing into a doorway two levels above.

Jack spun the cylinder of his six-shooter, took a deep breath, and dashed out the door. He scampered around a corner and vaulted to the top of a wall, then onto a roof. He slipped his .44 into the holster and began shimmying up a crumbled wall to the next level. A shot from above exploded a sandstone block in front of his face. He dropped quickly over the side of the wall, landing in a crouch and clawing at his eyes. He blinked a few times, clearing his vision, then crept to a lower portion of the wall and stuck his head up to look around.

Cash McCabe was clambering hurriedly along a narrow balcony above and to the left of Jack's position. Jack threw a shot at the outlaw as he ducked through a doorway.

"McCabe . . ." Jack shouted, "come on out. Let's finish this face to face."

No answer.

Jack skittered up the wall, then flattened himself against a dwelling and began inching across to where he had seen McCabe. He leapt onto the balcony and advanced toward the door into which Cash had disappeared. Pausing at the side of the doorway, he brought the hammer of his gun to full cock. He looked below and behind him, then stepped away from the side of the house.

A deafening barrage of thunder filled the cave as spears of lightning danced on the mesa top across the gulf of the canyon.

Gathering himself, Jack went head first through the door, rolling on his left shoulder and coming up off the stone floor in a crouch with his gun sweeping the inside of the room. It was empty. He looked up. Empty walls and bare timbers.

As Jack turned back to the door, the rattle of a stone from the top of a wall behind him jerked his gun hand around. The tiny room filled with the ear-pounding roar of a .45 and the acrid stench of gunsmoke. A bullet ripped into Jack's arm, spun him into the wall, to the ground, and sent his weapon skidding across the floor.

An evil, guttural laugh drew Jack Dancer's gaze to the cold, gray eyes of Cash McCabe—eyes filled with blood lust, fury, and a hint of madness. Cash inched closer along the top of the wall, his gun trained on Jack Dancer's heart, closing in for the kill. He extended the shiny barrel of the .45 to arm's length and closed one eye, squinting across the sight at his enemy below, prolonging the moment, savoring his conquest.

Jack scooted backward along the floor until he could retreat no further. His left hand touched something in the dust. The skull he had unearthed the day before. In desperation he grabbed the grinning head and hurled it at the gunman looming above him.

Cash McCabe ducked as the macabre missile flew past his head. He teetered, whirling his arms in circles to catch his balance. A booted foot slipped off the edge of the wall and he went hurtling over the side as a startled cry escaped his lips.

Jack dove across the room and palmed the .44 Colt in his left hand, then stumbled toward the door. A pounding pain in his arm staggered him and he grabbed for the frame of the opening to steady himself. He fought back the closing curtain of unconsciousness, shook his head, and looked around.

Cash was hustling across the stone courtyard below, dragging his left leg. Jack scurried after the fleeing killer, dropping off the sides of houses and over walls. He hit the cave floor and dropped to his knees. He waited for his head to clear of the spinning threat of blackness, switched the .44 to his right hand, braced his wounded arm with his left, and fired. The bullet tore the hat off McCabe's head and brought him around to face his adversary.

McCabe returned fire, backing away as the hammer of his gun fell again and again. Jack hugged the floor of the courtyard, the bullets striking around him and ricocheting off the stone of the cave floor and walls and houses like whining, angry hornets. The hollow click of Cash's cocking piece falling on an empty chamber brought Jack to his feet again. He advanced toward the man he had chased halfway across the western frontier.

Cash McCabe's features were twisted with fear as he fumbled desperately to fill the gun's empty cylinder while he shuffled backward across the cave floor, dragging his injured leg. A dancing display of sheet lightning beyond the cliff city rimmed his silhouette with a fiery light. He was brought up short as he backed against the low parapet at the cliff's edge. He raised his pistol.

The .45 in the outlaw's hand spat flame as Jack advanced slowly toward him, raising his own gun. Cash panicked and ducked, lunging to one side and falling out and over the wall.

It seemed to Jack, as he watched, that McCabe was poised in empty space—then he fell away and out of sight, screaming hideously as he bounced against the sheer, unforgiving face of the dark, wet cliff. Then it was quiet.

Clutching his wounded arm, Jack walked to the edge to look over. Cash McCabe lay in a twisted, twitching heap at the base of the glistening rock slab. The splintered, bleached gray stump of a dead piñon pine protruded from the gunman's chest, impaling him. The chase was over.

Jack Dancer rode into Durango leading a lineback dun with an empty saddle on its back. His right arm hung limp at his side, the sleeve of his shirt was stiffened and black with old blood. His eyes were rimmed with red, his jaw shaggy with a two-week growth of fine, ash-blond beard. He slumped in the saddle. Jack reined in the buckskin in front of a saloon, slipped to the ground, and tied both horses to the smooth log of the hitchrail. Then he crumpled onto the boardwalk.

The next recollection Jack had, he was lying between clean sheets on a feather mattress in a battered brass bedstead against a wall papered with old newspapers and broadsides. A smiling, porcine face hovered over his head.

"How you feelin' now, young fellow?" the face asked.

"Don't rightly know yet," Jack said. "Where am I?"

"Upstairs over the saloon. I'm Doc Bricker. This here's my room. I ain't really a doctor. I'm the barkeep downstairs. But I'm the closest we got to medical help in Durango at the moment. Our regular doctor caught a case of lead poison over a game of cards.

"I got you fixed up, though," Bricker said. "You ain't bad hurt. Just tore a chunk of meat out of your arm. No bones broke. No infection. You can get up if you're a mind to, though you're welcome to stay right there 'til you feel up to moving."

"Thanks. I best be on my way." Jack sat up. He laid back down again. "I'm a mite fuzzy. Maybe I will lay here a spell."

"You're Jack Dancer, ain't you?"

Jack nodded. "Yes. How'd you know?"

"Just figgered. Ever'body in Colorado knows how you been on the trail of them McCabes. I seen you brought in an extra horse. You get your man?"

"He sort of got himself, but he's dead."

Bricker nodded and smiled. "Well, you lay there and rest. When you get up, come on downstairs. I got beef and beans on the stove, and there's a fellow at the bar says he'd like to stand you a drink."

Jack looked surprised. He did not know anyone in this neck of the woods.

"Who would that be?"

"Old geezer name of Packrat Pete," Doc told him. "Been here since day before yesterday. Just made hisself some money, bettin' on which one, you or McCabe, would come back from the Mesa Verde."

Jack had a strange feeling of aimlessness now that his long quest for the McCabes had ended. Hunting the men responsible for the deaths of his mother and brother had been the compelling force in his life for a long time, driving him forward through each day. What now? Where was he to go, and what direction was his life to take? The chase was certainly not a thing to be enjoyed but, odd as it seemed, he felt let down now that it was done, bereft of a sense of purpose.

It was early on a Saturday night when he hit Telluride. High-pitched laughter and tinny piano music, played loud and off tune, rode shafts of yellow light out the saloon doors and into the night. The streets were swimming with celebrants in different stages of drunkenness and orneriness—

men desperate to have a good time after a full week of busting their backsides for miner's pay. Jack knew that the jubilance would take on a nasty edge as the night wore down, when the whiskey had brightened their eyes and dulled their brains.

A shot was fired in the street close behind him. The big buckskin shied, snorted, arched its back and crow-hopped around, almost unseating him. Jack gave it a whack on the jaw, choked up on the reins and turned it in on itself. The horse wheeled in a tight circle, shook its mane, and settled down.

Jack was hungry and tired, and he did not want to play cowboy, so he jabbed his heels in the horse's sides and angled through the milling crowd toward a livery. He parked the buckskin with a Mexican stablehand and returned to the street, walking, looking for a quiet place to buy a plate of almost anything that was hot and filling. He planned to have supper, then go to the doctor's office and check on John.

He passed two cafes where men were standing in line, waiting for a place at a table. Further down the block he turned into a small eatery called Wang Li's, squeezed between two saloons. He settled in a chair at an empty table as a tiny oriental lady, taking tiny oriental steps, came tripping across the sawdust-strewn floor with a large mug of steaming coffee. She handed him a laboriously hand-lettered bill of fare, then stood waiting. There was only one entrée available, beans and beef, with a choice of cornbread or sourdough biscuits. Jack smiled. He had expected something a bit more exotic. If not for the humble bean, he thought, the entire population west of the Mississippi would perish from starvation.

After he had eaten, he walked to the doctor's office, one block over, off the main street. The office was dark. He climbed the exterior stairway to the office door, wondering why every physician he had ever encountered was quartered on the second story. Seemed to him if a man was healthy enough to make it up a flight of stairs, he would not need the services of a doctor, anyhow. He knocked on the door but got no response. As he turned to leave, a man in the street below shouted up to him.

"You lookin' for the doc, he's over at O'Riley's playing cards."

Jack thanked him with a tug at the brim of his hat and headed for the saloon.

Entering the batwing doors through a fog of smoke, Jack squeezed and pushed and prodded his way across the crowded saloon floor to the poker tables, stopping where the aging frontier doctor who had tended John sat hoarding a fast-shrinking stake of gold and silver coins. The disgruntled physician cut his eyes up to take in the hovering interloper. Upon recognizing Jack, his frown faded and he answered the young man's unasked question.

"Howdy, son. John Dancer left out of here four days ago," the doctor told him. "Sam Coffee, the marshal over at Ouray, came by and invited him to stay with him and his missus until you got back. Said when you showed up to tell you to come on over."

Jack stayed the night in Telluride, treating himself to a hot bath, a store-bought shave, and a good night's rest at a rooming house. As the morning sun broke over the eastern peaks he was in the saddle, headed for Ouray.

As he rode, Jack talked to his horse. It was turning out to be a one-sided conversation, so after a few miles he settled back in the saddle to take in the splendor of the land around him. Breathing the thin, clear air stirring through the boughs of the great evergreens that forested the slopes was as heady as drinking strong wine. The branches of the trees were busy with thrushes, jays, orioles and wrens, diligently performing their daily chores of food gathering, joyous in their work, spilling forth sweet music to Jack's receptive soul. Lacy ferns with fronds as big as peach baskets graced the forest floor. Chipmunks and squirrels scampered across the mossy carpet and up and down the tall trunks of trees. Jack Dancer knew as he rode the skyline's backbones that he so loved life he wanted to live to be a hundred years old.

By late afternoon he was trotting his horse into Ouray. He pointed the buckskin down the rutted street toward the marshal's office.

As he passed the Tenkiller house, Jack tried not to look, but the memories drew his head around like iron filings drawn to a magnet. There were freshly laundered curtains on the windows and flowers blooming in a window box. He supposed that someone had moved in after Laura and Charlie left town.

He left his horse at the livery, telling the hostler to curry it and feed it a double portion of oats. Then he walked catty-corner across the street to Sam Coffee's office.

The door was standing open to admit the breeze. Sam was leaned back in his chair behind the desk talking to John Dancer, who was sitting on the plank floor, leaned against the wall, puffing on his pipe. They both looked up as he entered.

"Well, lordy. Look who's here. Took you long enough," John said. "I figured you'd gone and got yourself killed."

Then he came to his feet, grinning broadly. He threw his arms around his nephew, giving him a hearty hug. Jack flinched.

"What's wrong, boy? You hurt?" he asked, frowning with concern.

"Naw, it's nothing. Got a little hole where I'm not used to having one, is all. How are you doing, John. Had you ought to be up walking around yet?"

"Oh, goodness yes. I'm fit as a yearling."

Sam Coffee rounded the corner of his desk to shake Jack's hand.

"Good to see you, Jack," he said. "You two get caught up on what's happened. I'll walk over and tell the little woman to set an extra plate for supper."

The marshal walked outside and rounded the corner of the jail. As soon as he was out of sight of the office window, he picked up his pace and headed for the kitchen door of the Uncompahgre House.

Jack told John all that had happened since they had last seen each other—of the attempt on his life at the trading post, his fruitless search of the Lady Beth Mine and his subsequent meeting with Packrat Pete, and of his running gun battle with Cash McCabe in the lifeless cliff dwellings of the Ancient Ones.

John reached over and laid a hand on Jack's shoulder.

"When we started off together in Dodge City, you were a boy, Jack, and as green as spring grass. But you've grown to be a man . . . a man with the bark on, that I'm proud to ride the river with. Tom would have been just as proud . . . and your ma too, I think."

Jack's eyes misted over and he had started to speak when Laura Tenkiller came flying through the door and threw herself at him, driving him against the wall. With her arms wrapped tight around his neck, she covered his face with kisses. Jack finally pried her free to catch his breath, holding her at arms length and staring in surprised wonder.

"Laura . . . how . . . when . . . uh?"

"You notice that my partner," John said to Sam, who had followed Laura in, "is a silver-tongued, smooth talkin' sort of man. I taught him all he knows."

Laura kissed Jack hard once more, then wiped her eyes free of tears.

"We stayed two days in Denver after we left here, then Daddy said he was coming back with or without me. He got sick and tired of listening to me cry myself to sleep at night and watching me pick at my food." She laughed with the emotion of the moment. "Oh, Jack, I love you so."

He took her in his arms.

Just then Charlie Tenkiller walked into the office. He crossed to the young couple and wrapped his arms around them both.

"Oh," Laura said suddenly, pulling away. "The letter. Give Jack the letter."

Marshal Coffee reached across the desk and slid open the wide middle drawer. He withdrew a thick envelope and handed it to Jack.

"It's from Temple Houston," John told him. "I was going to open it, but your friend Coffee said he'd arrest me."

They all crowded around as Jack tore open the envelope. It contained a stack of legal documents and a cover letter from Houston.

"What does it say?" Laura asked expectantly.

"Well," he said, thumbing through the sheaf of papers, "there's a heap of legal gibberish, but what it comes down to is that Charlie here is a free man. A full pardon. You need never look over your shoulder again, my friend."

He handed the entire package to Charlie, patted the old Indian on the jaw and shook his hand. There were tears running down the half-breed's cheeks as Laura and Jack walked hand-in-hand out the door.

Epilogue

The quaking aspens were turning gold again when Jack and John Dancer rode back into Ouray. The wild horse gather had gone well and they had sold at a good price. There would be money enough to make their first year's payment on the land and to buy the materials they would need to start building the corrals and fences.

John had found the site for the horse ranch, twelve hundred and eighty acres of prime pasture land on the banks of the Gunnison. He and Jack had taken their proposition to the Centennial Bank in Denver and, as miracles sometimes happen, the president of the bank was the son of the old prospector the McCabes had murdered the previous year. They were granted the loan on the strength of their word and given a hearty "thank you" for ridding society of the family of killers.

Laura saw them coming and ran down the street to meet them. Jack leaned down and pulled her into the saddle behind him. She wrapped her arms tightly around his waist, gave him a squeeze, and laid her cheek against his back.

"Come in the house," Laura said. "Daddy has something he wants to tell you both. A big surprise."

Their boots were barely out of the stirrups when Charlie burst out the door waving a paper in the air.

"I done it," he shouted while hopping from one foot to the other in a gleeful jig. "Signed, sealed, and delivered. I sold my claim. A hundred and fifty thousand Yankee dollars!"

Laughing and yelling, they slapped him on the back as they filed in the door and through the parlor into the kitchen. The men gathered at the table while Laura put a pot of coffee on to brew.

"How'd you Dancer boys like to have a partner in that horse ranch of yours? I want to put this here money into the future before I drink it all up. You men run the ranch, I'll put up the capital for development. Three way partnership, what do you say?"

John looked at Jack and shrugged.

"What do you think, Jack? It would mean we could be in operation this fall instead of next year or the year after. I'm for it, I reckon."

"Fine by me, of course," Jack replied. "But are you real sure you want to do this, Charlie? You've not even seen the place."

"I'm sure," Charlie said, "sure of my new partners. But we can ride out there next week, the three of us."

"Wrong," Jack said, standing and pulling Laura close to him, "the two of you. Next week I'm going to be on my wedding trip."

John and Charlie were beaming proudly as they stood in their back broadcloth suits watching Mr. and Mrs. Jack Dancer board the Denver stage. Laura leaned out the window and tossed her bridal bouquet in their direction. The flowers hit John in the chest, but he held his arms wide, refusing to catch them.

"No, not me. I'm taking no such chances."

The driver whistled through his teeth and cracked the reins. The stage started with a lurch and a jangling of trace chains. John Dancer and Charles Tenkiller watched the coach down the street and around the bend out of town. John tore off his tie and stuffed it into his coat pocket, then slipped an arm around the old Indian's shoulders as they walked away.

"Partner, what say we get a bottle of firewater and take it over to your house. Maybe if I can get you drunk enough, I'll finally be able to win a game of checkers."

Cherokee Charlie let out a war whoop that shook windows a block away.